LEO RISING

ZODIAC GUARDIANS BOOK 3

TAMAR SLOAN
TRICIA BARR

Jess Connors
PUBLISHING

CASSANDRA

"Eat my dust, sucker!" Cassandra trills as she steers Princess Daisy into first place on the screen in front of her.

"I don't think so," says her cousin, Julia, right before shooting a red turtle shell at her.

Princess Daisy falters as she recovers from the hit, allowing Princess Peach to take the lead and cross the finish line first.

"No! I was so close!" Cassandra huffs while still wearing a smile. She looks at her cousin. "How did you get so good at video games?"

"I'm thirteen, it's kinda my job." Julia rolls her eyes with a giggle.

Cassandra reaches over and ruffles the top of Julia's head, messing up the smooth and shiny dark brown curtain that falls over her shoulders. Julia whines, but Cassandra knows she loves the attention. Julia practically worships her big cousin, and Cassandra enjoys being her role model. Julia may just be her favorite member of the family. These visits are the only times Cassandra gets to have fun at home.

"What's all the ruckus?" Her dad walks beneath the doorway, hands tucked into the pockets of his suit slacks, a disapproving frown setting his jaw as he looks down at them.

Cassandra stiffens and her smile deflates. She hadn't expected him home just yet.

She swallows, bracing herself. "I was just entertaining Julia with a video game." She shrugs, as if the gesture will afford her some forgiveness.

"I kicked her butt, Uncle Richard!" Julia squeals with glee.

"Did you really?" he asks Julia, though his eyes are trained critically on Cassandra.

She can almost feel herself shrinking under that heavy, judging gaze.

"Julia, why don't we get ready for dinner?" Cassandra suggests, desperate for an escape. "Nancy should be just about done."

Julia nods and climbs to her feet. "I hope she made peach cobbler again."

"Let's go see." Cassandra rises from the cushion she'd been using as a seat and attempts to guide Julia around her father, who remains standing in the doorway.

"Why don't you go ahead, Julia?" her dad says, placing a halting hand on Cassandra's shoulder. Cassandra flinches at the contact, then grinds her teeth, hoping he didn't notice. "I need a moment with my daughter."

Julia shrugs. "Okay." She skips up the hall to the dining room.

Cassandra's dad watches as the girl disappears around the corner, then turns his scrutinizing steel eyes on his daughter.

"Video games?" His tone is low and dark, making her spine go ramrod straight.

The all too familiar fear and shame ignite, and Cassandra clenches her fists at her sides.

It's alright, girl. Just breathe. Stay in control.

"She begged me, and I saw no harm in playing for a short while," she says, defensive. *Plus, I planned to stop long before you were supposed to be home.*

He steps closer, towering over her, forcing her to stumble backward. "No harm? Not only did you waste your time on frivolous games, but you *lost*, and to a child no less." He speaks in a whisper, his voice so hushed that the company in the kitchen wouldn't be able to hear.

Except it feels like he might as well be screaming at her.

Her palms tingle with the heat Cassandra's struggling to contain, and all she can do is press her nails into her skin, repeating her inner mantra. *Breathe. Stay in control...*

Her father narrows his eyes and leans in so that his shadow falls over her face. "I didn't raise a loser. Or did I?"

She shakes her head so forcefully that her blond locks whip around her face. "No, sir. I just thought letting her win would help boost her confidence."

He snorts, his nose wrinkling with a disgusted sneer. "One doesn't build true confidence by being handed anything. All you're doing is setting her up for future failure. She looks up to you, Cassandra, so show her someone worthy of such admiration."

"Yes, sir," she says, barely audible. Her grip is so tight that her knuckles are numb.

"Excuse me?" he hisses.

She clears her throat and repeats herself with more gusto, "Yes, sir."

Her father hovers in front of her, his gaze chipping away at her. She doesn't exhale until he finally turns around and walks to his study, closing the door behind him.

Cassandra backs all the way into her room, uncurling her fists and flexing her fingers. She looks down at her palms. Nothing is there but the four semi-circle indents, now with a fresh tinge of pink. Over the years, they've formed into scars, a permanent reminder of her dirty little secret.

She wipes her palms down her thighs, as if she could wipe away the shame. The motion makes her catch sight of her nails. She brings up her hands to inspect them.

Dammit.

Several of her nails have broken. She'll need another visit from Bing—that woman may be small and only know a handful of non-Japanese words, but she's a miracle worker with nail emergencies. And this absolutely is an emergency.

Cassandra pulls out her phone and texts the woman, requesting her help ASAP. Then she slips the phone in her back jeans pocket and looks up at the ornately carved French mirror hanging on the wall above her desk. She straightens her shoulders and tosses her hair over them, examining her reflection.

Golden locks that bounce perfectly with each step and frame her beautiful face like a halo. Amber eyes that shine like gems beneath her thick lashes, and lips so plump and pink they hardly need lip gloss. She's tall, thin, athletic, with enviable breasts and an ass you could bounce a quarter off of.

"You are perfect," she says to the gorgeous blonde looking back at her. At least on the outside, which is the only thing that counts. The only thing the world can see. "You are in control." She plasters on her winning smile and winks, then proudly walks out of her room to join Julia and the house-keeper in the kitchen.

2

TRISTAN

Swirling the red, orange, and yellow fro-yo flavors together, Tristan admits Veronica is onto something with her signature Sunrise Surprise. Sweet and tangy, the cold dessert slides over his tongue like daybreak over the horizon.

He can't believe it was only yesterday that he was here with the others. Celebrating. Trying to find a new middle-ground with Brielle.

Seeing the small sparks of light flicker along Cassandra's fingertips as she progressively became more frustrated waiting for her frozen dessert...

Tristan plonks the spoon into his half-finished cup, and his head sinks into his hands. They suspected Cassandra was a Zodiac Guardian from the beginning, until she was captured and tortured and she didn't protect herself.

Which means she either has some serious static electricity issues going on, or she's someone who can sure as hell keep a secret.

And the Zodiacs need to find out which is the case. Whether Cassandra is one of them.

Tristan pokes his fro-yo, the three colors are starting to blend into one, looking more like a dirty sunset. If only that was the hardest part of this next step forward. For that, he just needs to find a way to get Cassandra close to the stones and see whether one glows.

But before that, Tristan has to tell Brielle.

And he's never seen two people push each other's buttons as much as those two. It's quite possible Cassandra and Brielle *are* each other's triggers.

How can they defeat Chardis with two of the Zodiacs more focused on killing each other than Skins?

They can't, which is why Tristan's here, wasting precious fro-yo, wondering what he's supposed to do next.

He thinks back to the last few weeks. When Tristan and Jareth first met, neither of them were convinced they had much in common, and now they're roommates. In fact, it's kinda cool to have someone else rattling around in that giant house. Just this morning, they burned pancakes together, then took turns using them as frisbees. At each other.

Tristan sits up a little straighter. Brielle had tried to coordinate a meetup with the three of them not that long ago. She wanted Jareth and Tristan to meet, spend a little time together, get past the conclusions they'd drawn. And that's exactly what Tristan has to do with the girls!

He shoves away the fro-yo, excited that he has a plan. He just needs to find a way to get Brielle and Cassandra on talking terms. If Cassandra is a Zodiac, then surely the Zodiac bond will take care of the rest.

The cloying scent of too much perfume hits Tristan before Madge's voice does. "It's because you didn't have your usual gummy bears," she purrs.

Glancing down, Tristan realizes this is probably the first time he hasn't finished a fro-yo. In fact, the half that's left is turning into a melted puddle. "Probably."

Madge leans her elbows on the counter and slides forward. "I could make you one of my specials." She winks. "On the house."

Tristan scrambles to try and find a way to extricate himself. He can't guarantee that fro-yo won't be drugged.

"Excuse me. Are you Tristan?"

Glad for the distraction, Tristan turns to find out why a child is tugging on his shirt.

A boy, probably only eight, is standing beside him. He raises his hand, and Tristan sees that he's holding a thumb drive. "I need to give this to you."

Tristan smiles. "Sorry, dude. I think you must have the wrong person." Although it's weird that this kid knows his name. Tristan glances around the café, seeing that there's no one else here. "Do your parents know you're here?"

The kid frowns. "Just take it."

A little taken aback, Tristan finds himself doing as he's told before he's realized it.

The kid flashes him a grin, turns, and runs.

Tristan shoots to his feet. "Hey!"

But the kid's gone. Tristan glances at the thumb drive resting in his palm, wondering what's going on. Should he follow the little boy and demand some answers?

Madge leans forward even more. "Ooh, are you like a spy or something? Did someone just deliver top secret info that could take down the government?"

Tristan chuckles as he shakes his head. "Nobody wants me holding that sort of information. I can't decide on a favorite fro-yo flavor."

Madge winks. "You'll need to come back and try them all, then." Her eyes narrow in a way that Tristan thinks is supposed to look sultry. "Twice."

Getting up from his chair, Tristan holds up the thumb

drive as he grins. "Hopefully I'll have time, considering all my top-secret duties."

Madge giggles, a sound that's as youthful as her skin. With a jaunty wave, Tristan leaves the café, breaking into a jog the moment he's out the door.

He needs to know what's on the thumb drive.

He arrives home just as he's starting to breathe a little harder, pretty sure he achieved a new personal best. He steps around the pot of daisies beside the front door and passes his thumb over the sensor.

Inside, the scent of burnt pancakes still hangs in the air. Tristan pauses, but he can't hear Jareth in the kitchen or upstairs. He's either out with Veronica, or down in HQ.

Tristan makes his way to the bookcase, sliding back the photo of Zarius and Tess and noticing that the stab of pain doesn't feel so fresh. Not quite as deep. He brushes a thumb across the image, finding that the wishing is still just as raw.

He wishes he knew he was making them proud. He wishes he'd paid attention to Tess's waffle recipe.

He wishes they were here.

Pressing the barely visible button, the bookcase *whooshes* open. Tristan jogs down the stairs, shaking away the melancholy. He pulls the thumb drive out of his pocket, digging its sharp edges into his palm. The need to find out what's on it has become a steady burn.

He finds Jareth sitting at one of the desks, his cell to his ear as he smiles in an impressive imitation of Goofy. He straightens as he sees Tristan enter, speaking quietly into the phone. "I gotta go, the dude who burned my pancakes this morning is here."

Tristan rolls his eyes but doesn't comment.

Jareth hunches a little more around his cell. "Yeah, I love you, too."

Hiding his flinch in the same way he's been trained to

hide a punch, Tristan grabs his seat and rolls closer to his computer. He's glad Jareth's found what he has with Veronica. It looks special. Amazing.

Like a soulmate.

Ignoring that word, Tristan lifts the thumb drive to the port.

Jareth wheels over. "Watcha got there?"

"A kid gave this to me at Creamy Dreams, then disappeared faster than a perfectly cooked pancake."

Jareth frowns. "He just gave that to you and left? I don't like the sound of that. It's probably a virus."

Tristan pauses, the thumb drive hovering an inch away from the port. "Yeah, I've thought of that. Maybe some sort of trojan, maybe a way to trace us."

"And yet you're going to put it in?"

Letting out a slow breath, Tristan nods. The kid knew his name. "Someone wanted me to have this. I have to find out who."

"I'm not sure that's a good—"

But before Jareth can go all Mr. Risk Averse, Tristan shoves it into the slot. Instantly, a small red light starts pulsing on the thumb drive and his computer comes to life. The screen flickers, then turns blue.

Then nothing.

Jareth lets out a huff. "Well, you've done it now. I just unpacked the last of my books, too."

Tristan grits his teeth. If Chardis discovers their lair, there will be nowhere safe for the Zodiacs to go.

And Tristan had finally started calling this place, home, too.

Suddenly, the screen changes to white. Tristan locks his muscles, angling in front of Jareth. The thumb drive could be a bomb, for all he knows.

Jareth visibly jumps as words appear on the screen.

Virus scan complete. No threats detected.

Tristan and Jareth glance at each other and Tristan shrugs. "Alden was nothing if not thorough." They both turn back as more words appear on the screen.

Source unknown.

"Seems we've got a secret admirer," Tristan mutters.

The words change and Tristan's breath evaporates as he reads the first one.

Zarius.

This message was for his father!

Changes in dark matter. Wormhole being built somewhere. Chardis is up to something.

The screen goes black and they both leap back as the thumb drive bursts into flame. With a quick yank, Tristan flicks it onto the floor and stomps on it. The charred remains crumble, a small tendril of smoke rising into the air.

Tristan looks up to find Jareth's wide eyes on him. "Did that just say a freaking wormhole?"

3

BRIELLE

Truth is the core of Brielle's life. The focal point that all other matters revolve around. The glue that connects all things together.

She's used to hiding from the truths of those around her, bombarded since childhood by visions that expose the lies they tell. While she has made it her solemn vow to only speak the truth, she respects the right of others to make that choice. In fact, she rarely ever pries for information.

So, she sits in a rocking chair on the front porch, frowning over her current predicament.

Yesterday at Creamy Dreams, Tristan had been acting like he'd seen a ghost as he'd said, "I think there's another Zodiac Guardian right here in Mirror Point."

"What? Really? Who?" She'd matched his hushed tone, but she'd been unable to hide her excitement. Jareth and Veronica silently watched with anticipation for his answer.

Tristan had chewed on his lip, staring down at the table. Then he'd finally relaxed his features and shook his head. "I need to do a bit more research before I get everyone's hopes up. Make sure I wasn't just imagining it."

Brielle frowned, deflated. "What did you see?"

Tristan plastered a smile on his face and shook his head again. "I've been disappointed too many times. I'd better check it out first. Let's not worry about it right now. We're celebrating."

Jareth and Veronica had shrugged it off, and the outing had continued with laughter and jokes. But Brielle had been unable to let the issue go.

Tristan had seen something that rocked him so much it made him declare right then and there. He believed there was another Zodiac. Even if he doubted whatever it was, he should have shared the experience and gotten their take on it, right? That's what she'd done after meeting Jareth. If she'd never brought that up, there's no way Jareth would be a part of their team now. They'd have passed him by completely, and who knows if they'd have ever found him, especially if he'd fled, or worse, been taken by the Skins.

What could Tristan have seen in Creamy Dreams? And if it was potent enough to drain the color from his cheeks, why didn't she see it?

Oh, right. Because she'd been avoiding looking at him.

Because he said they couldn't be together.

Brielle knows that's in part why she's so obsessed about this. It's distracting her from having to deal with those feelings of rejection. Even though she understands why Tristan said no, it still burns like a sting from a giant cosmic scorpion.

She shakes away those thoughts and focuses back on the question at hand, the one she'd been pondering all day at school. Since he'd seen the prospective Zodiac Heir at Creamy Dreams, chances are he or she goes to Mirror Point High, so she'd stared holes in the backs and profiles of every student's head wondering if they were the subject of Tristan's suspicions.

There are ten more Zodiacs out there, waiting to be found. What if all of them are students here? She knows the likelihood of that is preposterous, but she still can't help but look at each face and wonder what their power might be.

"Bri? Are you out here?" Bea's searching voice snaps Brielle out of her musings.

She peers around the tall edge of the rocking chair to see Bea, her adoptive mother, opening the screen door. "Right here," she replies.

"Oh, good. Would you help me with dinner? I've got some pork chops I'm debating what to do with and I'd love your input."

"Sure," Brielle says, getting up and putting on a smile. "What about chicken-frying them and covering them in gravy?"

Bea smiles, hangs her head to the side and claps her hands on her thighs. "I knew it was a good idea to ask you. That sounds delicious, and Frank will love it!"

Brielle follows Bea into the kitchen and together they work on the food. Brielle prepares the egg mixture while Bea cleans the pork chops and pours bread crumbs into a wide-brimmed bowl for dipping and covering.

The two of them make a game out of cooking, laughing when the overly hot oil pops at both of them, and when they'd gotten distracted by conversation and fried one chop a little too long. This is why Brielle loves cooking so much. It's a completely liberating activity. It takes her mind off anything troubling her and gives her a tasty reward at the end. Even better if she gets to do it with someone she loves, and she does love Bea. It may not be the instinctive and powerful love a child has for its mother, not yet, but she does adore everything about Bea as a person, and she's sure her feelings will only grow in time.

"Oh, Frank called earlier and said the merger proposal

has been accepted," Bea says excitedly before placing a chop in the sizzling pan and springing her hand away from the popping oil. "All that's left to do is sign the contract."

And just like that, Brielle is brought right back down to Earth.

Brielle nods but says nothing, hoping her faltering smile goes unnoticed.

It doesn't.

"What's wrong?" Bea asks, her warm cocoa eyes falling on Brielle.

Brielle shrugs. "I just hope he reads the fine print, that's all."

Bea frowns, leaning against the counter. "You were acting strange at dinner with the Sinclairs the other night, and you hinted that you'd talk to me about it later but you never did." She raises her dark brows in a look that says now is the time to do so.

Brielle sucks in her bottom lip, unsure of just what to confide or even where to start.

"It's that girl, isn't it?" Bea asks, crossing her arms. "You know her from school?"

Brielle nods, then sighs. "We used to be best friends. She was at Grace Orphanage, too, when we were little. But after the Sinclairs adopted her, she changed. She's the epitome of a mean girl. Mirror Point's very own Regina George."

Bea shakes her head. "I thought I smelled a rotten egg through all that perfume. It's her eyes that give it away. When she smiles, her eyes don't."

Relief deflates Brielle's chest in a long breath. At least *someone* sees Cassandra's true colors, and Brielle's so glad it's Bea.

"And you're afraid that the apple doesn't fall far from the tree?" Bea asks, leaning her head forward in a discerning gesture.

"I just don't trust Mr. Sinclair," Brielle finally feels free enough to say, even if she can't confide her reasons.

"Well…" Bea puts her hands in the front pocket of her apron. "Frank is a very smart man, one not easily fooled. Have a little faith in him. If there's anything unscrupulous about Mr. Sinclair's dealings, he'll figure it out—Oh! Not again!"

She quickly grabs the tongs and pulls the dark brown chop out of the oil.

"We'll just have to make the gravy extra creamy," Brielle says, and they both giggle.

They continue to make the gravy and sauteed vegetables, and Brielle feels lighter. It's nice to know she can talk to Bea about sensitive topics. She's never had that before, and it feels so good.

Maybe she's wrong about Mr. Sinclair. Maybe he's not the villain of this story, and maybe Cassandra has had a perfectly nice childhood.

All Brielle can do is hope that this business deal isn't as nefarious as she fears.

CASSANDRA

"Wow, top of your class? That's great!"

Cassandra almost squirms under her Uncle George's praise as she sits across from him at dinner. She smiles, and part of her, some deep part, soaks up his affection like a sponge. But her overall reaction is discomfort, and disbelief. Is he really proud of her accomplishments, or is he just putting on a show? The same way that her father did when he heard of Julia being accepted into the Honor Society at her elementary school or making a field goal in soccer.

"Your dad told me that you just took the SATs," Uncle George continues. "How do you think you did?"

Cassandra shrugs, prodding her roast beef with her fork. "The scores are supposed to come in any day now."

"I'm sure you'll get an A!" Julia shouts, admiration sparkling in her hazel eyes.

Cassandra giggles.

"The SATs isn't that kind of test," Cassandra's father corrects, his voice devoid of amusement. "There are no letter grades assigned, only a number, and that number determines one's entire future. I expect Cassandra will get a perfect score."

Cassandra swallows, then finally takes a bite of her roast beef as an excuse to avoid the steel gaze she can feel on her cheeks.

"Regardless of whether or not you get a perfect score"— Uncle George flares his fingers in air quotes—"there's an opportunity I've been meaning to propose to you."

Cassandra looks up at him mid-chew, giving him her full attention.

"Are you still interested in getting into law?" he asks.

Uncle George is debatably the best prosecuting attorney in the state, which, for New York, is saying something. His firm handles several dozen high-profile cases at any given time, and he's even made the newspapers a few times. When she was younger, her mother had taken her to watch one of his cases against a popular hip-hop artist, and Cassandra had been so impressed with how eloquently and stealthily he debated. He'd won the case, and she's admired him ever since.

She'd always told herself that she could help her father's business from a legal standpoint. She could defend him if the need ever arose—and it had a few times already.

"Yes, I think it would be a wonderful career path for me," she says as she slices off another bite of juicy brown meat.

Uncle George chuckles. "Well, an internship position just opened in my office, and I would be delighted if you would take it."

Cassandra can't stop her lips from spreading in a wide smile, her chest ballooning with excitement.

"It won't pay much, but it would look great on your college resume and give you valuable work experience for whatever path you decide to take."

"That sounds great, Uncle George!" Her animated gaze

darts from her uncle to her father, and like his eyes are lasers, the dark look on her father's face bursts her bubble with an almost audible *pop.*

She instantly sobers.

"I'll definitely think about it," she says. "Not sure I'll have time around track and my other extra-curriculars, so I'll see what I can do."

The wobbly curve to her uncle's lips and the way his eyes falter down to his plate say that he caught on to whatever weirdness just passed between Cassandra and her father. She needs to change the subject.

"Have you heard from Aunt May?" she asks Uncle George. "Are she and Mom having a fun trip?" Her mom and aunt went on a cruise in Central America to celebrate her aunt's fortieth birthday. Cassandra's mom hasn't responded to any texts, and Cassandra's assumed that cell service is just out wherever they are.

"Oh yeah, she calls us every night," Julia chimes in, her voice muffled by cheeks full of potatoes. "They got to climb a pyramid!"

Cassandra's chest flattens with the sinking of her heart. Aunt May has called her family every night, but Cassandra's mom can't be bothered to answer a single text…

"That's cool," Cassandra says, lifting her cheeks in a hollow smile. "I'm glad they're having a nice time."

"You know, George," her dad begins, and she looks up to see a pensive expression on his face. "I'm so glad you brought up the idea of an internship. I hadn't thought of it before, but my office could definitely use one."

Cassandra's ears perk up as her heart trips in hopeful anticipation. Is he actually going to ask her to intern for him?

He turns his thoughtful, calculating eyes to her. "Cassandra."

She holds her breath.

"The Pierces' daughter, Brielle... Do you know if she has an afterschool job? I think she might be the perfect candidate."

Cassandra's hopes plummet faster and harder than a ten ton anchor. A fierce heat burns in her palms, and she has to grip the sides of her thighs like iron presses to hide the glow she's sure is there.

"Brielle?" She doesn't even try to cut the edge of disgust from her voice.

Her father knows full well who Brielle is, and how much she digs at Cassandra's nerves. After the dinner with the Pierces, they'd discussed her new parental situation and their past experience with her, and Cassandra had taken every opportunity to cut her down.

How could he even be considering *Brielle*?

"Yes, she's a sharp girl, Frank tells me," he says casually, as if he can't see the hurt and anger behind Cassandra's eyes. "She might be just the person to help our firm thrive, especially now that her father is going to be a partner."

Cassandra shakes her head. "You *can't* be serious." The heat from her palms is practically scalding her thighs, and she tries to focus her mantra in her head through the outrage. *Breathe. Stay in control. Damn, Brielle!*

He narrows his eyes at her. "Do you think I would joke about something as important as my business? Do you think my business is a joke?"

Cassandra's spine stiffens as she realizes her mistake.

Never question him.

The sudden absence of heat has her thighs feeling chilled. Or is that just the look in his eyes.

She shakes her head. "Of course not. I just don't think she would be a good fit for the office." She tries to pass a dismissive giggle and rolls her eyes. "I've gone to school with that girl my whole life, and she's not as smart as she seems."

Cassandra knows this is a lie, that Brielle is possibly too smart for her own good, but she'll say anything to dissuade her father from making this blatant and massive mistake.

"Thank you for your concern, Cassandra, but I'll be the judge of that," he says.

The rest of the dinner passes in awkward silence, her mantra a constant chant in her head as she tries to keep the heat at bay, sitting on her hands like that will help. She dreads the evening's end as Uncle George and Julia prepare to leave.

"See you tomorrow?" Julia asks as she shrugs into her coat by the front door.

"Of course," Cassandra says, hugging her with arms that don't want to let go.

"Can we play Mario Kart again?" Julia whispers, stealing a glance at Cassandra's father behind her.

"We'll see," Cassandra whispers back even quieter, then winks.

Julia's smile spreads wide.

And then they leave.

The silence in the house is so fine, Cassandra can hear the soft pad of her father's shoes on the carpet as he moves to the front door.

And locks it.

The *click* of that little knob is deafening, and Cassandra flinches. She wants to run to her room, to barricade herself in and escape what she knows is coming. But like the good daughter she is, she stays perfectly still, waiting.

"You will not go to work for your uncle," he says, his voice low but full of authority.

Her throat contracts several times as she tries and fails to swallow. "I was just being polite about his offer. I know my academics come first. And honestly, I'd much rather work for you. Brielle is—"

"How dare you contradict me," he snaps, rage simmering in his dark eyes. "Especially in front of company. Especially in front of *him*."

Fear spears down her spine. "I'm so sorry, sir," she stammers in panic. "It's just that I—"

"You thought you know better than I do, is that it?" He steps closer, his fingers pulling the end of the leather belt at his waist to release the buckle.

She stumbles backward. Her head is shaking back and forth so rapidly, she could give herself whiplash. "No! Of course, not."

"I think you need to be reminded of your place," he hisses as he pulls the belt completely free.

"No, please," she whimpers, backing into the wall. "I promise I'll never question you again."

"I'll make sure of that."

The belt comes down, and Cassandra withdraws inside herself, digging her nails so deep into her palms that all the pain becomes white noise.

Maybe this time, his fury will be over in just a few lashes.

5

TRISTAN

"Can he even do that?" Jareth asks, a hint of panic in his voice.

Tristan rakes his hand through his hair. "I don't know." He holds Jareth's gaze. "I think so."

"But you're not sure?"

Yep, definitely a thread of panic in there.

With a sigh, Tristan pushes up from his chair, the need to pace zinging through his body. He can't blame Jareth for freaking out. The message wasn't exactly full of hope.

Changes in dark matter.

Wormhole being built somewhere.

Chardis is up to something.

"I only know what Zarius told me," Tristan says, trying to keep the edge out of his voice. "But as you know, dark matter essentially makes up most of the Universe, it's just that humans only know of it theoretically."

Jareth nods. "Yep, you explained that to me. Humans haven't been able to detect it yet, just prove its existence mathematically. Basically, things like gravitational effects can't be explained unless more matter is present than can be seen."

Glad that Jareth was paying attention, Tristan's pacing picks up. "But to more advanced humanoids out there"—he points to himself and Jareth— "dark matter has been proven. And through some sick twist of physics, somewhere, somehow, dark matter gained sentience."

"Chardis," Jareth says darkly.

"Yeah. Chardis *is* dark matter. He can make it do whatever he darned well wants."

Jareth stills, and Tristan looks away. Chardis's ability to manipulate dark matter is how he killed Zarius and Tess. All he had to do was contract the matter holding together the cells of their hearts...

Shoving away the memory before it can shred him all over again, Tristan clenches his hands. "As far as we can tell, he wants to use that power to take over the Universe and rule the galaxies."

"For what end?"

Tristan blinks. Of course, Jareth would ask another question he can't answer. "We never found out. I suspect it has something to do with the fact it will make him the most powerful being in the Universe."

Jareth crosses his arms. "And I'm guessing wormholes are made up of dark matter."

Tristan shrugs. "They'd have to be, just like everything else in the Universe."

"So, it stands to reason that Chardis could manipulate one."

Jareth says the words more as a statement than a question and Tristan's glad he doesn't have to answer. It would've been a rhetorical one, anyway.

The buzzing energy is suddenly gone, and Tristan flops back into his chair. "Yeah. We could have a situation..."

"We don't know who sent the message, do we?"

Tristan shakes his head. He should've followed the boy, tried to get some more information out of him. Namely, who wanted to make sure he knew this? "The bottom line is, we can't afford not to take it seriously."

Jareth spins around to his computer screen, typing quickly. He squints at the screen as he scrolls through the information that he brought up. "From what I can tell, a wormhole is a tunnel with two ends in different points in space." He glances at Tristan. "It says a wormhole could connect extremely long distances such as a billion light years or more, short distances such as a few meters, or different Universes."

Different Universes.

"So, if the message is true, Chardis is creating a shortcut."

Tristan wants to drop his head in his hands, but he stops himself. Jareth needs him to be strong right now.

Tristan blinks. Just like Zarius was for him.

"I can see why you miss Zarius," Jareth says quietly.

Tristan winces, although he's not surprised at Jareth's perceptiveness. They both live with the grief of losing their parents.

But not only did Tristan lose his father, he lost his guiding light. Which means it's up to him to be that for the Zodiacs, now.

Straightening his shoulders, he levels Jareth with an unflinching gaze. "He believed in the Zodiac Guardians, and so do I."

Jareth wipes his hands down his face. "I suppose that's something."

Tristan wheels over on his chair so he can slap him on the back. "That's the attitude we're looking for!" Shoving off, he zips back to his desk. "First things first, we need to find out everything we can on wormholes."

They have no idea what Chardis could be sending through his interstellar shortcut.

Jareth turns back to his own screen. "My mother would've liked you," he murmurs.

Conscious of the compliment he was just handed, Tristan grins at Jareth. "She sounds like a wise woman." He sobers. "If she knew the truth about you, would she have believed in the Zodiacs?"

Jareth's response is instantaneous. "There would've been no doubt in her mind that good would prevail over evil."

Tristan nods, his smile back. "Yep. A wise woman."

Jareth shakes his head, his own lips twitching at the edges, but before he can say anything, his cell rings.

Tristan rolls his eyes. "Oh, Jareth," he chimes in a terrible falsetto imitation of Veronica. "It's been, like, twelve minutes. I miss you!"

Jareth glares at Tristan as he picks it up. "Hey."

Although he doesn't use Veronica's name, his voice takes on the husky edge it always does when he's talking to her. Tristan blows him a kiss and flutters his lashes.

Jareth spins so his back is facing him. "What's up?" His spine straightens so fast Tristan wonders how it doesn't give him whiplash. "He's what?"

The alarm in Jareth's voice has Tristan stilling. He watches as Jareth hunches over once more, as if he's wrapping himself around his cell phone. It's a protective move, a worried move.

Jareth nods several times but doesn't say anything. Uneasiness slithers it's way up Tristan's spine, wondering if this has anything to do with Veronica's father, Jack. He'd hoped the truce they established when McNally was captured would've lasted a little longer...

Turning back to face Tristan, Jareth raises his gaze. His eyes are wide, and the panic that was twisting in them earlier is back. "Hang on a sec, Tristan's right here." Jareth angles the phone away from his mouth but doesn't lower it. "Something's happened."

Something worse than a wormhole forming somewhere near Earth? But Tristan doesn't ask the question. No point in wishing more trouble for the Zodiacs. Instead, he waits, hoping Veronica called to say she had a fight with her older brother or something.

"McNally's escaped."

Tristan shoots to his feet. "What?"

"Looks like it was an inside job sometime during the night. He's still at large."

In a blink, Tristan's pacing again. McNally's a Skin. One of Chardis's assassins. And he's going to have a personal vendetta with the people who put him behind bars. The three Zodiac Guardians he wants dead.

And Veronica.

Tristan stops, facing Jareth. "Go get her. Now."

Jareth is on his feet before Tristan's finished. He lifts the cell so he's talking into it again. "I'm coming, Veronica. I'll be there in ten."

He sprints for the door, his face tight.

Tristan watches him take the stairs two at a time. "Remember, don't use your suit if you don't need to," he calls after him.

The last thing they need right now is for humans to discover the existence of the Zodiacs.

Jamming his hands through his hair again, Tristan wonders how Zarius didn't go bald.

Then again, Zarius didn't live long enough to meet other Zodiacs. Or to learn that it would mean Chardis stepping up his game.

A wormhole doing who knows what.

A dangerous Skin who knows too much about them on the loose.

Tristan yanks his own cell out of his pocket. There's one person he needs to make sure is safe. One person who he needs here with him.

Brielle.

6

BRIELLE

All through dinner, Brielle had been jiggling her leg, debating the best way to approach the topic of merge specifics with Frank. It had been a light-hearted meal, as many are in the Pierce home, and Frank had graciously taken the overdone pork chop and smothered it in a pool of gravy. They laughed about the face he made with his first bite, and laughed even harder at his weak claims that it was perfectly fine.

But now dinner is over, and Brielle finds herself hovering outside his office, waiting for the perfect ice-breaker to just pop into her head.

Finally, she decides that such a thing isn't going to happen and bites the bullet with little for a plan.

"Hey Dad, whatcha workin' on?" she asks as she strolls in as casually as she can manage.

He turns around, blazing that same smile that always pops up whenever she calls him "Dad."

"Oh, just going over this contract for the merger," he says.

Perfect.

"You know, um, I was hoping to talk to you about just

that," she says, eyes still roaming the room as she puts her words together. "Are you totally sure this deal is a good one?"

He frowns in curiosity. "I really think so. This could be very good for our company. Why do you ask?"

She can't tell him about her first encounter with Mr. Sinclair, she'd already decided that.

"It might sound kinda weird, but...I get these senses about people sometimes, and they're usually right on the nose." She purses her lips, her mind getting too fuzzy with nervousness to grab hold of the words she wants.

"And you have a bad feeling about Mr. Sinclair?" Frank guesses.

"Yeah," she admits. "I just wanna make sure that—"

The doorbell rings.

Both Brielle and Frank glance at the clock on the wall. It's five after eight. Who would come all the way out here at this time? Tristan would have at least texted before showing up.

"I'll get it," she offers, heading for the door and wondering if Tristan might have smashed yet another phone during a training session with Jareth.

She opens the door, but the tall, dark and manicured figure on her doorstep is the last person she expected.

"Ah, Brielle, just the young lady I wanted to talk to." Mr. Sinclair's voice is smooth as velvet, but with a sinister ring that she can't shake. He holds out his hand. "Lovely to see you again."

Not one single part of her wants to shake his hand. Her skin retracts as if he were something vile, contagious, explosive.

Ignoring his offered hand, she takes a few steps back from the doorway. "Sorry, let me get my dad."

"Actually, I was hoping to make you a proposition, as well as speaking to him about the contract," he says, putting one foot inside the doorframe.

"Me?" she asks, putting her hand against her chest.

"Yes. You see, I've been considering opening up an internship position in my office," he explains, coming all the way inside despite her lack of invitation. "I feel that, especially with this merger, you might be an excellent candidate."

"Me?" she asks again, her pitch more shrill this time. "Why not ask your daughter? Surely Cassandra would be better suited."

He chuckles dismissively. "Cassandra's ambitions are…elsewhere."

Suddenly, the edges of her vision blur, then spiral inward with an urgency that doesn't allow her to brace herself for the twisted rollercoaster ride she's being sucked into.

Guilt, disgust and rage coalesce like waves in a sea storm, forcing themselves upon her like Mr. Sinclair's very presence. But worse than that is the memories she's helpless not to bear witness to. His memories.

Starring Cassandra.

Strike after strike, the crack of his belt as it smacks against the skin of her back that's barely protected by a thin shirt. Cassandra, cowering on the floor as each blow makes her curl up tighter and smaller. The fear in her teary eyes and cries muffled by hands clasped to her mouth, and the sick satisfaction the image elicits in the man whose eyes Brielle's seeing through.

More visions flash, flicker in and out of time and space. The setting changes. A different wall, different floor, sometimes a bed. And Cassandra ages in reverse, becoming younger and younger. But the scenario remains the same. Cassandra balled up in pain and terror, as her adoptive father beats her until he's satisfied.

Using all the willpower she can muster, Brielle wrenches herself from the vision before it reaches its end, absolutely unwilling to witness any more.

"Ah, Richard, what are you doing here?"

She hears Frank's voice, sees him approaching from her peripheral vision, but all she can do is stand in the same spot, holding the door open and staring blankly. The guilt twists and contorts in her belly and chest like a creature from *Alien*, threatening to burst out any second and cover Frank and Mr. Sinclair in horrifying gore in its eagerness to devour its originator.

"I wanted to see how you were coming along with the contract," the despicable man says to Frank. "And to offer your daughter an internship with our firm."

"Really?" Frank turns a surprised gaze to Brielle.

But she can't really see him. All she can see is Cassandra's humiliated face. The belt coming down. The bruises and welts and angry red flesh.

"She hasn't yet responded." Mr. Sinclair turns expectant steel eyes on Brielle. "What do you think?"

Not only no, but pitch no, never in a million years, over my dead body, not even when Hell freezes over or pigs fly.

"Excuse me," she says, putting her hand to her mouth as the sting of bile claws at the back of her tongue. Without another word, she runs to the bathroom, slams and locks the door, and reaches the toilet just in time to hurl her partially digested pork chops into the porcelain bowl.

Poor Cassandra!

Deep down, Brielle always knew. Of course, she'd never thought twice about the long sleeved shirts Cassandra would randomly wear in the middle of summer. Or the way she'd snap at a girl friend who'd hug her the wrong way in the halls. Under all that sass, hatefulness, perfume and perfect blonde hair, Cassandra was hiding the evidence of her father's abuse. All this time!

Overcome by the motley crew of dark and dirty

emotions, tears flood over Brielle's eyelids and down her cheeks.

I failed her. I was her best friend and I failed to save her from this monster!

Brielle weeps, stifling her sniffling attempts to breathe through the sobs so as not to alert anyone to her unexplainable sorrow.

"Bri, is everything okay in there?" Frank says, rapping on the other side of the door.

Brielle wipes her eyes and moistens her lips until she can speak. "Uh yeah, probably just had a bad pork chop. I'm fine."

"Okay, I'll be in my office with Mr. Sinclair if you need anything." He lingers a moment, then his footsteps fade down the hall.

Her phone vibrates in her pocket, the steady repetitive pattern telling her it's a call. She pulls it out to see Tristan's name on the screen. She swipes the answer button.

"Hey, what's up?" she asks through her tight throat.

"Emergency meeting at HQ," he says, the sound of his voice putting her on edge. "I need you here asap."

Automatically, she replies, "I'll be right there."

She can only imagine that whatever reason Tristan had for calling the meeting can't be good, but she's honestly looking forward to anything that could give her escape from Mr. Sinclair's presence, from the visions.

From the knowledge that Cassandra's in trouble, and it's all her fault.

7

CASSANDRA

Curled up in her bed, wrapped in a heavy comforter, is the only place Cassandra feels safe. When she's here, it means the worst is over, and as long as she lays on her side, the welts on her back don't hurt as much. She can almost pretend they aren't there.

Why did she have to open her big mouth? She should know better than to say anything that contradicts or opposes her father. Hasn't she been through this enough times to have learned by now?

Yes, she has. But he mentioned *her*. The one person who Cassandra can never seem to shake. It's hard for Cassandra to control her emotions whenever Brielle's around, or any time someone even says her name. And for her father to consider her for an internship, or to consider her at all, over Cassandra... There's no greater trigger.

Her hands tremble as they pull the comforter tighter around herself. The heat has completely vanished from them, left them limp and ineffective. Nevermind the lashing she just endured, which always makes her feel helpless.

Not just helpless because the one person who is supposed

to be loving and nurturing to her is the one causing her so much pain, but because of the knowledge that she can't deny whenever her palms burn—that *her dad* is the one in danger from *her*.

She closes her eyes, determined to put this night behind her and wake to a bright new day full of possibilities.

But when sleep finally does come, she finds that the night isn't done with her yet.

"What do you think they'll look like?" asks six-year-old Brielle as they lay on their bellies at the ends of their beds, looking at each other in the darkness. Lights out at Grace Orphanage didn't have to mean they had to sleep.

"I don't even care, as long as they love me," Cassandra says, the void in her heart aching. "But it would be nice if they have blond hair like me so I could pretend they were my real parents." She twirls a lock of gold around her index finger.

"I'm sure they'll love you, Cassie, no matter what," Brielle says, smiling sweetly. "You're the best person I know." She reaches her small hand across the distance between their beds, and Cassandra takes hold and squeezes.

"Maybe we can find someone to adopt both of us," Cassandra says hopefully, gently swinging their clasped hands. "Then we could really be sisters."

"That would be amazing!" Brielle squeals. "But even if that doesn't happen, you'll always be my sister."

"And you'll always be mine."

With a start, Cassandra's eyes pop open. There's a searing in her chest, like a freshly stitched wound has just been ripped apart.

Only this wound has been here for a decade, never to be mended.

Cassandra had truly loved Brielle then. She had firmly believed that they would always be best friends. Sisters, as Brielle had promised.

Until the Meet and Greet that changed everything. Cassandra couldn't help but feel a twinge of jealousy as she watched the Sinclairs take to Brielle and walk through the garden with her. They had been talking to Cassandra when they first arrived, but as she always did, Brielle charmed them with her sweetness. At the time, Cassandra had believed that Brielle hadn't been trying to steal their attention, but now Cassandra knows better.

Then when Brielle had ruined her chances with them, and they chose Cassandra instead, Brielle tried to make sure Cassandra didn't get a family, especially not one that rejected her. The whole thing had hurt so much. How could Brielle betray her like that? She tried to steal the same family *twice!*

And the things Brielle had said about the prospective father were ludicrous.

When Cassandra first came home with the Sinclairs, they were everything she'd ever wanted. Her father tucked her in every night and read her bedtime stories. Her mother filled her closet with the prettiest dresses and always fawned over Cassandra's long golden hair, trying a different updo for every outing. Brielle had been so wrong.

Until the first time Cassandra made her father upset.

She had cried all night long after the spanking. She'd never felt more degraded or less human, and the shame that filled her was unbearable. *This doesn't prove anything*, she'd told herself. *It's not unheard of for parents to spank their children. I will just never disobey him again, and this won't ever happen again.*

But it did happen again. And again. And again. More and more often. And as she got older, the spanking turned into whippings with his belt, so that no one would ever question his puffy hands.

There had been one time he smacked her in the face. She'd gotten a black eye and a busted lip, and he'd kept her home from school until it healed, telling the office that she was sick with a flu. That had been the only time there was any outward proof, and the only time her mother had questioned it. Her father had told her mother that Cassandra ran into a doorknob, and that if they didn't keep her home from school, people would get suspicious just as she did. Her mother had bought it. She always believed everything he said. His word was law in their house.

She probably could have told her mother the truth then. Or any number of times. But what good would that do? Her mother wouldn't have believed her, and even if she had, the most likely outcome would be that, after investigations and legal stuff, Cassandra would end up right back in the orphanage, without a family.

Things had been so perfect in the beginning. There had been no question then that her parents loved her. But as things got worse and worse with her father, she had to face the truth: that the rumors about Brielle at the orphanage were true. Everyone said she was a witch. That she brought bad luck to people. That she knew things she shouldn't; Cassandra had witnessed that a few times herself. The only explanation for how quickly things went bad was that Brielle had somehow cursed Cassandra's father. She had accused him of being abusive, and had somehow made it true.

Facing that fact gave Cassandra another harsh realization. What if, through some form of witchery, Brielle discovered Cassandra's secret? The one she'd been keeping clenched away her entire life? Brielle could expose Cassandra as the freak she really is, and Cassandra would lose everything— her friends, her home, her family, as well as any hopes of ever finding another family to adopt her again.

Once Cassandra realized this, she'd decided to act preemptively. If she could defame Brielle to the point that no one liked her or would ever believe a crazy word she said,

Cassandra would never have to fear exposure. And it wasn't like Brielle didn't deserve it for what she did.

Brielle was the enemy, and Cassandra made sure that everyone around them knew that. Before long, Brielle was an outcast, and Cassandra's secret was safe.

But there was always the poor sad sap who would wander by and get sucked into Brielle's web. Adalind Shaw, but that girl was a real weirdo. They kinda deserved each other. Then Tristan, and now Jareth? Two perfectly good hotties who, despite Cassandra's best efforts, are under Brielle's spell. Admittedly, Cassandra doesn't know much about Jareth, but she knows that Tristan doesn't deserve whatever Brielle is planning for him. She can't just leave him in her claws. It's Cassandra's civic duty to save him from her. Even if he doesn't end up with Cassandra, which would be a nice bonus, at least he won't end up with Brielle.

Very gingerly, she arches her back to roll over in bed and makes a promise to herself. She needs to get back into prevention mode, do everything she can to save those she cares about from Brielle's bewitchment. And right now, that's Tristan and her dad.

Cassandra smiles and closes her eyes.

When she's through, Brielle will once again have no one.

8

TRISTAN

The band around Tristan's chest unwinds when he sees Brielle enter HQ. She's okay.

She's safe.

She stops at the bottom of the stairs and her gaze instantly connects with his. His heart jolts like it always does, a sensation he welcomes as much as it doesn't make sense. Brielle quickly looks away and continues to scan the room, taking in Jareth and Veronica sitting close together.

Her brow creases as she registers they're all here. "What's up? It sounded urgent."

Tristan indicates her usual chair by one of the desks. "We've had some news."

Veronica does the impossible and shifts closer to Jareth, a move even Brielle notices. Her frown scrunches down another notch as she sits.

Tristan stands, shoving his hands in his pockets as he wonders where to start. Everything's changed in the space of a few hours.

He clears his throat. "Some things have happened. Firstly, McNally's escaped."

Brielle's eyes widen. "He's what?"

Veronica tucks a strand of hair behind her ear. "It only happened a few hours ago. He killed three guards and held the other at gunpoint, forcing him to open the locked doors." She looks away. "Then he killed him, too."

White hot rage bubbles in Tristan's veins. McNally's killings have already started. Who knows how many others will die as he tries to find the Zodiacs.

Brielle's hand flies to her mouth. "He's going to come looking for us."

Tristan has to lock his knees as the need to go to her overwhelms him. He presses the soles of his feet to the floor, imagining them melding with the cement. "Which means we need to be ready for him."

Brielle's sweet features set in determined lines. She nods. "Of course. And we will be."

Tristan grins, impressed at how quickly she's taking this in her stride. "Damn right, we will be." He turns to Veronica. "You'll keep us posted as any news comes up?"

She rolls her eyes. "Kind of like I just did with McNally escaping?"

"Basically." He pauses. "Thanks."

Tristan knows that means Veronica has essentially become a spy against her own father. That's no small ask.

And a testament of how deep her love for Jareth is. And of her support for the Zodiacs.

She grips Jareth's hand more tightly. "My dad is going to do everything he can to catch him. McNally will probably be back behind bars before we know it."

Tristan doesn't answer. The feds are the ones who let McNally escape in the first place. Not to mention, Jack never realized that evil had infiltrated the FBI...

Tristan stills as another thought hits him. With McNally gone, does the fragile truce Jack agreed on even hold? Is

Tristan going to have to deal with Jack breathing down his neck, on top of everything else?

Shoving the distasteful thought aside, Tristan decides he needs to focus on the issues at hand. He glances at the others. "Until McNally is dealt with, we need to stick together as much as possible. Always in twos, never alone."

Jareth wraps his arm around Veronica's shoulder. "Consider it done."

Tristan suppresses an eye roll of his own. He doesn't point out they're already joined at the lips.

He turns to Brielle, ignoring the little spark of joy the words he's about to say spark. "If you're not with your parents or at school, then you're with me."

Brielle blinks. "Ah, sure." She straightens her shoulders. "We should probably train more."

Tristan nods, his throat tight. Even with Jareth and Brielle there, those hours after school are the sweetest torture Tristan has ever experienced. Sparring with Brielle is exhilarating. Fun.

Excruciating.

She leans forward. "You said firstly. There's more?"

Wishing the note of caution in her tone was unwarranted, Tristan nods again. "I was given a message today, one meant for Zarius. It said Chardis is manipulating dark matter." He sighs. "He might be growing a wormhole."

Veronica gasps, the news a first for her, too. "As in a black hole out in space somewhere? To do what?"

"We don't know, nor do we have the technology to trace it, but we do know he's getting closer and stronger."

HQ fills with heavy silence, and it feels as if Chardis's presence is far closer than Tristan hopes. He jams his hands back in his pockets, hating that there's no plan to respond to this threat.

Even if they knew where the wormhole is, how do they

close it? And what will manage to get through before they do?

Or who...

Brielle chews on her bottom lip in thought. "We need to find the next Zodiac Heir. Soon."

Tristan's gut clenches. She's right. It's the only way they'll become stronger.

Her moss green gaze traps his. "You said you thought you'd found one?"

"You did?" Jareth asks in surprise.

Tristan turns to look at him, finding it much easier than Brielle's trusting, perceptive gaze. "I thought I did."

Veronica frowns. "And?"

Except Tristan can't say anything unless he knows for sure. The last thing their team needs right now is upheaval.

And Cassandra would be upheaval.

She could possibly tear apart every hard-won connection they've forged.

He clenches his hands. "I need a little more time before I point any fingers." Three mouths open at once, and Tristan quickly continues. "You're going to have to trust me on this."

They snap shut, one by one.

Jareth is the first to speak. "Time isn't something we have a lot of, but we're not a team without trust. I can wait."

Veronica nods. "Me, too. I've always said my boyfriend is wise beyond his years," she adds solemnly.

Tristan looks to Brielle last. If she insists, he'll tell her. There's enough unwanted strain between them without adding lies to it.

But surely the double sucker punch the news has dealt is enough for one day.

Hopefully she realizes he's doing this for her.

Inexplicably, her lips tip up. "I trust you."

Tristan's own smile is reflexive. They're working as a team. "I suggest we start reading up on wormholes, then."

But as everyone turns to their respective computers, Jareth and Veronica huddled around his, Tristan lets the smile die.

They're working as a team.

And yet, they're facing more challenges than they ever have before.

JACK

17:13

"Cadbury!"

Jack clenches his jaw at the way Flanagan barks his name. Like the order it is. Like Jack has no choice but to come running.

Wishing he'd popped an antacid so he has something to grind apart from his own teeth, Jack stands and yanks on his jacket as he approaches Flannagan's office.

McNally's old office.

The boss's office.

Even though Flanagan is younger than Jack.

Even though he's not that great an investigator.

And he didn't crack the McNally case.

But Flanagan doesn't openly talk about alien invasions, which ended Jack's chances of promotion a long time ago.

He stops in the doorway. "Yeah, Flanagan?" Jack refuses to call him Sir.

Flanagan's thin lips press together so hard they practically disappear, but then his gaze flares as he glances over Jack's shoulder. "I'd like you to meet Clara." His lips appear again so they can curl up in a smile. "Your assistant on the McNally case."

Jack spins around to see a woman, not as young as Flanagan, but not as grizzled as Jack, striding toward them. He narrows his eyes. With dark hair in a tight bun and a navy pants suit, she's pretty but professional.

She holds out her hand. "I've heard a lot about you, Agent."

Jack stops his mouth from twisting. He has no doubt she has.

Clara smiles tightly. "I'm looking forward to catching the bastard."

Jack shakes her hand, noting the strong, confident grip. "Nice to meet you." He turns back to Flanagan. "I'm sure she'll be a fabulous asset. Maybe she can pair up with Dawes. Or anyone else in the team."

Five of them have been appointed to get McNally back. The Bureau knows they can't afford to have the Triple Murderer out on the loose. It's only a matter of time before the media gets a whiff of this.

Flanagan snorts. "I need someone with you. Someone with a level head."

Someone who isn't going to say the word 'aliens.'

Jack ignores Clara as she stands behind him. "I've got this," he bites out.

Flanagan's lips are in danger of disappearing again. "You and Clara sure do. She's been transferred because she's a sharpshooter. Between the two of you, I'm expecting to see results." He picks up a file and raps it on the top of his desk. "That's all."

Jack spins around and almost crashes straight into Clara. She steps back just in time, and Jack mutters an apology as he strides away. Except the sounds of her heels are right behind him.

Not stopping until he gets to his desk, Jack spins around. "Look—"

Clara jams a file into his chest. "I've reviewed the security footage from the correctional facility. McNally does an impressive Houdini act."

"Yep." She's not telling him anything he doesn't know.

"The moment he's out the door, it's like he…disappears."

"Yep."

McNally was filmed walking around the corner of the building like he was out for an afternoon walk, not a criminal on the run. He should've appeared on the next camera that covers the south end of the prison, but he's not.

It's like he disappears into thin air.

"Look, Jack—is it okay if I call you that?"

Not really. "Sure."

Clara flashes him a smile and Jack notes her straight, white teeth. "Great, thanks." Minimal makeup. Probably knows she doesn't need it. "I'm going to spare you the whole 'life's hard in the FBI as a woman' spiel, and just say that this case could be a career maker for me. I'm going to do what it takes to catch McNally."

Conscious that he was just being one of those agents who define Clara by her gender, rather than whether she's a decent investigator or not, Jack flips open the file she passed him. Flicking through the pages, he sees it's a pretty comprehensive summary of what they've got so far.

Which is very little.

"What's your take on it?" Clara asks.

Jack doesn't look up. The only way McNally escaped is if he isn't human, but Jack knows not to say that out loud. For all he knows, Clara has been sent to babysit him. Well, let her try to find some reasonable explanation.

He's going to find out the truth.

Jack passes her the file with a shrug. "Your guess is as good as mine."

Clara takes the file and drops it on his desk. "So, we're hitting the streets? See if anyone's seen our perp?"

Picking up his now-cold coffee, Jack heads to the elevator. That's exactly what he was going to do. Alone.

"I'll keep you post—"

He snaps his mouth shut as Clara strides past him, reaching the lifts before he does.

Jack sighs, jamming his free hand into his pocket so he can grip the bottle of antacids in there.

Trying to find who McNally really is just got harder.

9

BRIELLE

The buzz in Brielle's mind is so loud, she can't focus in English class.

Yesterday, she'd only had one question to ponder: who's the next Zodiac? Today, the questions pile so high, she can't dig herself out. What can she do to protect Frank from Mr. Sinclair's potentially shady dealings? What are the Zodiacs going to do about the wormhole and Chardis's imminent next move?

And most of all, as Cassandra's sitting a few rows in front of her, what is she going to do to save her best-friend-turned-arch-nemesis?

Brielle still doesn't understand why Cassandra hates her so much. If Cassandra really has been abused all this time, then she's always known that what Brielle warned about was true. That Brielle wasn't trying to ruin anything for Cassandra, but was really trying to save her from that fate.

Could it be that Cassandra resents Brielle for failing to save her? Or for being right, when all Cassandra wanted was a loving family, which she thought was what she was getting?

And whatever the reason, how on Earth is Brielle going to even begin to make amends and actually help her?

For so many years, she's just wanted to get away from Cassandra's relentless bullying. But now that she knows the trauma behind that perfect barbie face, all she wants is to get closer, to erase whatever damage that's been done. Looking at the back of Cassandra's head now, she doesn't see her tormentor of the past ten years. She sees her childhood best friend desperately in need of help.

And Brielle is going to help her whether she likes it or not.

The bell rings, and students vacate their desks and file toward the door. Fueled by compassion, Brielle pushes through the crowd and follows Cassandra out into the hall. She looks for the right moment to stop her, for the right words to break this fragile yet impenetrable ice.

To Brielle's relief, Cassandra veers toward the bathrooms and pushes inside. Taking a deep, fortifying breath, Brielle goes in after her.

Cassandra stands at a sink in front of the wall-to-wall mirror, dabbing at her thick lashes with her fingertip. Amber eyes catch Brielle through the mirror, and narrow as the barbie-doll body they belong to pauses and tenses.

"What do you want?" Cassandra asks with a sneer.

The tone of Cassandra's voice still makes the hairs on the back of Brielle's neck stand on edge, but her overall hostility no longer ignites the same fury.

"I was hoping we could talk," Brielle says, keeping her tone friendly and open.

"About what?" Cassandra smooches her lips as she regards her reflection again.

Here goes nothing. "About the marks on your back."

Cassandra freezes, her stick of lip gloss slipping through her fingers and clattering on the tiled floor.

It seems an eternity passes that they both stand there, frozen in time. Cassandra looking like a deer in the headlights as she stares blindly at her reflection, and Brielle floating on a little cloud of hope that, this time, she reaches her.

But all too quickly, the eternal second passes, and Cassandra turns fiery amber eyes on her like they would burn Brielle alive if they could.

"Okay, you wanna talk?" Her whole body angles in Brielle's direction, a lioness who's just spotted a wounded gazelle. "Let's talk."

Brielle feels too much like that wounded gazelle, too immobilized to escape and knowing it's too late anyway.

"My father has offered you an internship with his company," she says as she stalks closer. Her mascaraed eyes narrow as she hisses, "You will *not* accept it."

Brielle is taken aback. She'd completely forgotten the proposal that had brought the horrifying and heart-wrenching vision with it.

"Of course, not!" Brielle exclaims in disgust that can't be masked.

The predatory look on Cassandra's face turns to outrage. "Oh, what, now you're too good for my family?"

Brielle shakes her head nervously. "No, that's not it at all." Not in those exact words, at least. "I just—"

"Save it." Cassandra puts an obstinate hand in front of Brielle's face. "I'm done letting you ruin my life. And I'll be damned if I'm going to let you take down anyone else I care about."

Scrunching her face in confusion, Brielle stammers, "W-what are you talking about?"

Cassandra points a pink-polished finger an inch from Brielle's nose. "I'm onto you. I have been from the day you tried to ruin my adoption. You've turned my dad's head with your dark magic, but I will not let you mess up anyone else's life. I will make sure that you end up alone. Count on it."

And before Brielle can say anything edgewise, Cassandra storms out of the bathroom just as the second bell rings.

"I just want to help you!" Brielle calls after her.

But it's too late. Cassandra is long gone and didn't hear a single syllable.

What just happened?

Tristan is tense and quiet in cooking class and Brielle's almost glad. Just like last night at the meeting, she doesn't want to have to explain the secret she's struggling with. Mostly because it's not her secret to share. It's Cassandra's. Brielle would be further betraying that broken friendship if she said a word to anyone.

But doesn't the secret need to be shared with *someone*? Like Social Services?

Brielle already knows the answer to that. Cassandra would know, now, that it was Brielle who'd said something, and she'd never forgive her. Because Cassandra would lose the family she has, even though it's not the one she deserves.

This whole thing is tearing Brielle apart. How can she help someone who wants nothing to do with her? What's that old saying? You can lead a horse to water, but you can't make it drink? This is one stubborn horse who absolutely does *not* want to drink.

For a moment, she considers that Tristan would probably have some good advice on the matter. Telling him would certainly ease her mind. But he's so weighed down by this message about the wormhole, and she doesn't want to pile on more. It would be selfish of her to speak a word of it. And she's still carrying the weight of Mr. Sinclair's guilt, which is almost too agonizing and disgusting to bear.

She's relieved when second period is over, if only for the distraction of having to walk to her next class.

And that's the way the whole day goes until lunch. Seeing Jareth and Tristan already sitting under their tree on the lawn is her saving grace. She's loved hearing their back-and-forth banter the past week as new roommates, and it promises to be the ultimate mental palette cleanser.

Except that Jareth can read Brielle like a large print children's book.

"What's up with your face?" he asks, his mouth half full.

"Huh?" She turns away from her yet-to-be-bitten sandwich. "Oh, just…thinking."

Jareth shakes his head. "I swear, it's like the two of you are the same person sometimes. And I thought I was supposed to be the silent brooding one."

"Not since Veronica," she and Tristan say in unison, and it's the first time she's laughed in days.

"See, same person." Jareth throws his hands up. "Uh-oh, here comes trouble," he mutters, rapidly looking away into the distance.

Curious eyes have Brielle looking in the direction he just turned away from, and why is she not surprised to see Cassandra sauntering toward them?

"Hey, Tristan," Cassandra purrs as if neither Brielle nor Jareth are even there.

She's got the look of a girl on a mission, and dammit if it isn't a good look on her.

"What's up?" Tristan asks, his handsome face still furrowed with the echo of brooding.

"I was hoping you and I could work on the English assignment together," Cassandra says, all charm and charisma. "I'm having the hardest time wrapping my head around allegories with this Beowulf story."

Brielle expects him to politely reject Cassandra's offer. His plate is so full that Brielle knows he can't put any significant focus on school work.

But something shifts in Tristan's face, a glint in his eye that Brielle can't translate.

He smiles. "Actually, that's exactly what I was hoping. I'm struggling, too, and it would be nice to bounce ideas off someone. Can you come by after school?"

Cassandra's smile is both triumphant and arrogant, like she already knew she'd get her yes. "Of course."

"Great, I'll text you my new address," he says, his winning smile in full bloom, and Brielle is struck dumb by the enigmatic turn of events.

"See you then," she says, right before shooting Brielle a taunting glare.

"Did you seriously just invite Regina George to our bachelor pad?" Jareth asks, and Brielle chokes on the shared simile with just a hint of glee.

Tristan shrugs with what Brielle can tell is faux nonchalance. "That English assignment is a killer."

Jareth leans forward and cocks his head at Tristan with a confused expression. Then he glances at Brielle and finally shakes his head. He puts up his hands. "Whatever you say. I'll be with Veronica, minding my own business."

The boys go back to chowing down on their food, and Brielle isn't sure how she feels about this situation. She gets the sense that Cassandra is acting on her threat, to turn everyone against Brielle and leave her with no one.

But Brielle knows that won't work on Tristan. On the contrary, Tristan might be able to alter Cassandra's perspective, if they get close enough. But at the same time, anyone else getting close to Tristan, especially that close, rubs Brielle the wrong way.

Baby steps, she tells herself. She, Tristan and Jareth are an unbreakable team. Getting close to one means getting close to all. Brielle just has to have faith that this study session will be a good thing.

Even better if she could tell Tristan, but her guilt won't let her.

Ah, pitch.

TRISTAN

Tristan watches the screen as Cassandra pops her lipstick back in her bag on the other side of his front door. She fluffs her hair, dividing it and flicking it forward over both shoulders. He sighs, wondering how long this is going to take. Surely, Cassandra knows she's pretty enough that she doesn't need to go to these lengths...

Finally, she rings the doorbell. He doesn't think he's seen Brielle fluff her hair once. She's never seemed to care for makeup.

And yet, she's still the most beautiful girl he's ever seen.

Shaking the thought away as he heads down the hall, he opens the door with a grin. "Hey, Cassandra."

Her lion-colored eyes light up at the sight of him. "Hello, Tristan," she purrs.

Stepping back, Tristan lets her pass. She flashes him a cheeky wink as she passes, and he's not sure whether he should grin harder or shake his head.

He leads her to the dining area, where he's already got some drinks and food set up. He lifts up a bottle, "Mineral water," then the plate beside it, scrunching up his nose, "and vegetable sticks."

Cassandra's eyes widen. "You remembered?"

He shrugs. "I'm good with details."

Sitting down, Cassandra lets her bag flop to the floor. "But you remembered."

Taking the seat across from her, Tristan smiles even as he makes a mental note that this has had such an impact on Cassandra. "That's what friends do."

Cassandra blinks and a second later she leans forward, her top gaping a little to reveal creamy flesh. "Or someone who could be more…"

Tristan shakes his head ruefully. "I admire your tenacity, Cassie, but—"

She frowns as she yanks back. "Don't call me that." Before he can wonder about that, too, or think about apologizing, Cassandra grabs her bag. "So, allegory and Beowulf, huh?"

Taking her cue, Tristan flips open his notebook. He's already half-finished the assignment, but as much as he hated accepting Cassandra's invitation to study right in front of Brielle, it was too good an opportunity.

He needs to know.

Cassandra brings out the book itself, flipping through it. "So, have you read it?"

Tristan's mouth turns down. "Yep, how can a poem be three thousand lines long? That's two and a half hours of my life I'll never get back."

She giggles. "I know, right?"

Glad they're back on smiling terms, Tristan pours her a glass of mineral water. "It's all very good versus evil, isn't it?"

"Yes, I noticed that." Cassandra glances at her notes. "Whoever wrote it really humanized evil. It's both an omniscient black threat and at the same time, just a part of being human."

Impressed with her perceptiveness, Tristan angles his head. "What do you think? Which is more true?"

He watches her response closely, conscious she could be talking about the time the Skins captured and tortured her.

Cassandra looks away. "Some people definitely have evil in them," she says quietly. She takes a sip of her mineral water before looking back at him, pasting a smile on her face. "Overall, I'd say it's a story of family, fate, and loyalty."

Once again, a perceptive summary. "Quite the trifecta, huh?"

Cassandra's glossed lips twist. "None of them give you much choice, do they?"

"Loyalty's a choice," Tristan points out. "You just have to decide what you're fighting for."

"Like Brielle?" she asks, her voice suddenly hard. "You back her up, no matter what?"

Tristan draws back a little. Cassandra needed this study session about as much as he did, so why is she here? Just to try and get to Brielle?

He decides to get to the heart of this. "Brielle and I aren't a thing," he states matter-of-factly. They never can be.

Cassandra's lips thin. "Good."

"Why?"

"She'll break your heart, Tristan. She acts sweet and innocent, but…she has a dark side."

Tristan shakes his head. "Don't we all?"

She frowns fiercely. "Some more than others. Look, Tristan, I like you and I don't want to see you hurt. I also don't want you believing anything she says about me"—her frown intensifies—"or my family."

Curious, and a little concerned, Tristan leans forward. "Brielle hasn't told me anything. If she does know something, she's keeping it between you and her."

Cassandra's mouth pops open only for her to quickly

snap it shut. "That's exactly how she plays it—acts trustworthy, then betrays you."

Which brings them to the crux of the issue. Some deep-seeded wound exists between Cassandra and Brielle.

Tristan glances at the box casually sitting beside the carrot sticks.

Cassandra might be one of them.

"Can I trust you," he asks quietly.

Something flickers in Cassandra's gold eyes. "Of course, you can."

Tristan grins. "Great! Because I need your opinion." He draws the black box closer to him. "My parents left me these, and I have no idea whether they should be in a safe somewhere."

Cassandra blinks at the change of topic, but quickly recovers with a smile. "Sure, my mom has quite the jewelry collection. I might be able to give you an idea."

"Awesome." Tristan flips the lid open, then stills as the gems catch the light. His eyes are instantly drawn to the second tanzanite cushioned in the center and a thought hits him. One he can't believe he didn't think of before.

What if Cassandra's the other Gemini? His twin? His soulmate?

The one person whose powers will meld with his so they can defeat Chardis.

He didn't think of it because he doesn't want it to be true. He wants his soulmate to be someone else...

Tristan flips the box around, not sure which outcome he wants more.

For Cassandra to be a Zodiac Guardian.

Or for her to be human.

"Oh, they're beautiful," Cassandra breathes.

Looking almost mesmerized, she reaches forward, her gaze trapped by one gem. The citrine.

She bypasses the others, totally focused on the smooth yellow stone. But just before she reaches it, Cassandra jerks her hand back, her fingers curling tightly into her palm.

But not before Tristan sees it.

The citrine stone glowed. Trembled.

It found its master.

Sweet pitch, Cassandra is the Leo!

Cassandra shrugs dismissively as she tucks her hands in her lap. "They look lovely. I'm sure they're worth a lot of money."

"Yes, I'm pretty sure they're priceless," Tristan murmurs as he closes the box, wondering what he should do next.

"Oh my goodness," Cassandra says as she glances at her watch. "Is that the time?" With quick movements, she packs up her belongings. "Sorry, I have an…appointment."

Tristan doesn't need Brielle's powers to know that's a lie, but Cassandra's already striding to the door.

"Thanks for the study session, it really helped," she lies again, smiling over her shoulder.

Tristan follows, feeling a little shell-shocked. Cassandra's running, but from what?

"No need to show me out," she trills chirpily. "I know where I'm going."

With a megawatt smile, she's gone, clicking the door shut behind her.

Tristan stands in the hallway, knowing he should follow her, but not finding the ability to move. Cassandra is one of them.

And yet, this is the first time he's hesitated when he's discovered another Zodiac. He has to tell Cassandra. She needs to know.

But somehow, he also needs to get Brielle and Cassandra on speaking terms.

To have them fighting on the same side.

Before any decisions can be made, Tristan's cell rings. Glancing at it, his brows contract when he sees it's a silent number. Probably a telemarketer…

Swiping the screen, Tristan lifts it to his ear. "Yes?"

"Well, hello, Tristan."

Ice spears down Tristan's spine as he recognizes the voice.

McNally.

JACK

17:56

Jack's run out of antacids, and his stomach is letting him know it. The two hotdogs he got from the street vendor haven't helped, either.

What makes it worse is he has nothing to show for the new hole burning in his gut.

He and Clara have spent half the day walking the streets of LA, their concentric circles getting bigger and bigger as they expand beyond McNally's last sighting.

And they've found zilch.

Jack's tired of the blank looks each time they show McNally's photo. The distrustful glares every time they approach another homeless person hunched on a street corner. The flash of hope when someone says they recognize the image, except that the man was wearing a tutu and fishnet stockings…over his mermaid tattoos.

"Meet you back here tomorrow morning?" mutters Clara.

Impressed with her determination, Jack nods. "Yeah, I'll bring the coffee."

"None for me, thanks. Caffeine tastes like mud."

Jack couldn't agree more, but that doesn't mean he's not going to drink several a day.

Clara huffs as they start to make their way back to the car. "He couldn't have disappeared into thin air." She hesitates. "Could he?"

Jack glances at her, wondering how much she knows about his theories. "What are you suggesting?"

She shakes her head ruefully. "Sorry, I'm sounding like a crazy person, not a respected FBI agent."

Jack winces just as his foot hits a garbage bag sitting beside a trash can.

"Hey, watch it!"

He steps back, instantly on alert as he watches the garbage bag unfold. The layers peel back, revealing a grizzled old woman wearing one like a poncho.

"Sorry, ma'am."

She sneers at him. "I'm tired of people like you treatin' me like trash."

Jack keeps his brows where they are even though they desperately want to hike up as Clara crosses her arms beside him. The woman is dressed in black garbage bags from head to toe.

"My apologies." He's about to keep walking but he stops, holding up the photo of McNally even though it's a long shot. "Have you seen anyone who looks like this?"

The woman barely glances at it. "Yep. Earlier today."

Jack wonders what McNally was allegedly wearing this time. "Oh? What did he look like?"

"Like a suit who treats people like trash," spits the woman through brown teeth. "He was over there." She lifts a plastic-covered arm to point to a phone booth across the road.

"He was making a phone call?" Excitement tingles along Jack's skin. This could be a lead.

"I'm pretty sure he wasn't Superman, cause he didn't come out in blue Lycra, so yes, I'd say he was making a phone call."

"Thanks," Jack says dryly. He pulls a note out of his wallet. "Here, so you can get more garbage bags."

The woman snatches the bill out of his hand in a flash. "The thick ones are expensive, you know," she mutters as she curls back into herself, once again becoming the trash she accused him of treating her as.

Jack turns to Clara and she holds up her cell. "I'm on it. I'll find out what calls were made from the booth today."

Jack nods a thanks and Clara paces away, already dialing. Glancing at the phone booth, Jack wonders if they're finally getting somewhere. Seeing that Clara's deep in conversation, he pulls his own cell out, pressing the familiar buttons. Veronica picks up after the second ring.

"Hey KitKat, just letting you know I'm going to be home a little late."

"You found anything?" Veronica asks, sounding a little tense.

"We might have something, it's too early to tell." Jack can't blame her for being on edge, having a serial killer out on the loose makes him nervous, too. "You might want to order pizza."

"Cool, I'm with Jareth," Veronica says lightly. "I'll probably have dinner with him."

Jack frowns. "I'm not sure I like the sound of that."

His daughter sighs. "I told you, Dad. Jareth was just in the wrong place at the wrong time."

"Because some organization is hunting Tristan Ayers and McNally was associated with them…"

"Exactly," she says brightly. "And they thought—just like you did—that Tristan and Jareth were connected somehow. But as it turns out, Jareth's one of the good guys." Veronica says the words slowly seeing as she's repeated them so many times.

"So no news on this organization?"

"I'm still working on it. I'm just not that close to Tristan, yet. And we need to honor this truce…"

Jack grinds his teeth. He hates that darned truce. "And you said Jareth's living with a friend." He rubs his forehead. "The place had better be safe," he warns.

"I'm fine, Dad. Jareth's friend is loaded and his house is practically a fortress. You just focus on catching the Triple Murderer."

They hang up, and Jack stares at his phone, not sure why he feels unsettled. Is it because they haven't been able to figure out what this mysterious organization is? Or because it feels like his daughter is keeping something from him…

"One call was made."

Jack looks up to find Clara standing in front of him. He stills. "And?"

"Like the woman said, about an hour ago." Clara glances at her screen. "McNally phoned someone called Tristan Ayers."

The name slams through Jack, and at the same time, it doesn't surprise him. Of course McNally was calling Tristan. Which also means Veronica's intel could be true.

Jack nods curtly. "I'll look into it."

Clara opens her mouth only to snap it shut again. Jack is the lead investigator on this case, so he calls the shots. Spinning around, he heads back to the car. The moment he's alone, he has one more phone call to make.

Tristan will want to talk to him about as much as Jack wants to talk to Tristan, but it seems they have a common enemy.

11

CASSANDRA

Cassandra's hands are shaking as she opens her front door, and they feel hotter than ever.

What just happened?

She and Tristan were chatting and flirting, and everything was going so well. Then he opened that box full of large precious gems, and something changed.

That princess cut citrine had been so beautiful, so alluring. Cassandra had always fancied herself a diamonds kinda girl, but she'd never seen anything more gorgeous or tempting than that sunshine yellow stone.

The one that begged to be touched.

But when she'd reached out, it had felt like raw electricity shot up her arm and radiated through her extremities. No, not electricity. Pure energy. Hot and potent. And now it was all she could do to keep her hands from glowing. She'd been afraid they'd melt the steering wheel as she drove home.

She rushes through the house to her room and digs through her drawers in search of a pair of gloves. It's not cold enough for mittens, but the curiosity at her wearing them will be far less traumatic than her dad seeing her darkest secret literally shining from her tightly clenched fists.

"You're home late." Her dad's voice in the doorway behind her startles her into dropping the black gloves she's just found, and she even more desperately picks them back up and shoves her hands into them before turning around.

"I had a study session with a friend over a paper for English," she says, trying to keep her voice steady as she casually holds her hands out of sight.

"Why did you need it?" he asks, his voice dripping with criticism as always.

She shrugs, feigning disinterest. "I didn't, but he needed the help." She notices her mistake after it's already too late.

"He? You were studying with a boy?" His eyes are like daggers, glinting silver and sharp.

"He's nothing, Daddy," she says in a rush to cover her tracks. "Just a friend who clearly needed help from the top student in the class."

"Yes, but you're not the top student in the class anymore, are you?" He steps into her room with menace.

"What are you talking about?" she asks, this time truly stymied by his accusation.

He crosses his arms. "I checked your class ranking on the school's website, and you're no longer in lead for valedictorian."

A lump grows in her throat. "Wha-bu-who is?" she stammers.

His eyes narrow. "The Pierces' girl, Brielle. I knew I was right to choose her for an intern. You're turning out to be quite the disappointment."

How is she going to get out of the beating that is clearly imminent? Isn't the shame of Brielle outdoing her yet again enough? She can't take it, not today! Not with her hands searing through her gloves.

The sound of the front door opening and closing is followed by a gleeful, "I'm home!"

Her dad backs away and leaves the room, eyes full of promise that this isn't over, but Cassandra's never been more grateful to hear her mother's voice.

Cassandra waits in the hall for her father to briefly greet her mother and peck her on the cheek before disappearing into the kitchen. Fueled by cooling relief, Cassandra runs down the hall and throws her arms around her mother. The hug is responded to with a platonic pat on the back, but Cassandra doesn't care. Her mother's presence is enough. It means she's no longer alone with her father and his harsh judgment.

"How was your trip?" Cassandra asks when her mother pulls away.

"It was heavenly, but the flight home was exhausting!" Her mother collapses onto the loveseat, looking over-dramatically drained. Then her eyes fix on Cassandra's hands. "What's with the gloves?"

Cassandra automatically shoves her hands behind her back. "Oh…just trying a new moisturizing treatment."

Her mother raises a dubious, finely-plucked brow, then looks away, indifferent.

Cassandra sits on the armchair catty-corner to the love seat. "Did you take any pictures? I'd love to see and hear about what you did. Julia said Aunt May told her about a Mayan pyramid. I—"

"Oh, not now, dear," her mother says dismissively. "I really am too tired. All I want is a long warm bath and a decent night's sleep. We can talk about the trip tomorrow."

And before Cassandra can say anything else, her mother is up and gone down the hall.

All too familiar emotions bear down on her as she sits alone in the living room.

Why did she let herself care? She'd missed her mother so much over the past two weeks she's been gone, letting herself believe that the feeling was mutual, despite the lack of return calls or texts. She let herself think life would somehow get better when her mother came back, forgetting how empty it had been before she left.

But the truth echoes around her in the large and sterile living room, too loud to ignore.

Her mother doesn't care, and her father's care is so strong it hurts.

Why can't she just be loved? They used to love her. She knows they did.

And maybe, just maybe, if she tries harder to be better, they'll love her again.

"Why are you such a disappointment!" her dad hisses as he strikes his belt down against her bare back.

She curls tighter into a ball, which only makes her unprotected flesh more accessible. Without clothes, the pain from the impact is searing, like it cuts right down to her soul.

But why is she naked? What happened to her clothes?

"Why can't you be better?"

WHACK!

"We should have adopted Brielle."

WHACK!

"Maybe then we'd have a daughter we could actually be proud of, and you'd be someone else's problem!"

"Stop!" she screams.

Cassandra opens her eyes to see that she's sitting up in

her bed, beads of cold sweat covering her entire body and soaking her sheets.

With stunning relief, she realizes it was just a bad dream.

And yet her back stings as if it had really just happened. Old wounds brought to life by memories and promises of tomorrow.

She lifts her hands to run them over her face and wipe away the sweat, but a sight too shocking for words has them freezing half way up.

She must still be dreaming. She has to be!

This can't be happening. Not again!

Staring wide-eyed at her opens palms in front of her, she can't deny it. This is real life.

Her black gloves have almost completely burned away, the woven fabric barely hanging to the tops of her fingers by charred fragments, and the glow from her palms is casting her dark room in soft yellow light.

This is getting out of control. She can barely contain the heat during the day, always believing sleep was her one escape. But now clearly even that isn't true.

What is she going to do?

She thought she was past this, that she'd gotten a handle on it. She can't afford another accident. Not now.

A memory she'd shoved into the deepest recesses of her mind years ago bursts through its mental chains and replays like an old movie.

Back at the orphanage. She was only four. One of the older girls, Shelly, had been picking on her for weeks. A chubby, freckled girl who probably hated Cassandra for her blonde hair and pretty face. She'd chased Cassandra into the gardens when everyone else was inside getting ready for dinner.

"You're so stupid, Cass," Shelly taunted. "You think

anyone will ever want a stupid little brat like you? You'll never get adopted."

Shelly had cornered Cassandra against the hedge of rose bushes and shoved her to the ground.

Fear was quickly replaced by anger, and Cassandra jumped to her feet and pushed back.

But it wasn't just force that left Cassandra's angry hands.

A burst of light erupted from them and threw Shelly clear across the garden, tendrils of it sparking off around her and igniting the flower bushes. Faster than Cassandra could question what happened, the entire garden went up in flames. She'd run to Shelly, trying to wake her, but the girl's whole chest and face was bloody and steaming, burned by the explosion. She would not wake.

Oh god.

Cassandra had killed her!

Alarmed shouts from the windows triggered Cassandra's flight instinct, and she ran as fast as she could away from the scene.

Soon the whole orphanage was in the yard, the nuns desperately trying to put out the blaze. The paramedics and firemen arrived and distinguished it, carting Shelly off on a gurney.

As it turned out, Shelly hadn't died. She'd just been badly burned. She spent months in the hospital, and Cassandra had later heard that one of the nurses had adopted her.

For years, Cassandra had tried to convince herself that it hadn't been her doing. That it had been some freak accident. The paramedics had found matches and a lighter on Shelly, and the fire had been chalked up to her arsenious tendencies.

But as time went by, and the heat in Cassandra's hands only grew, the truth could no longer be ignored.

She'd burned Shelly.

And if she's not careful, she's going to hurt someone again.

Most likely her father.

She shakes her head adamantly.

No, she's not going to let that happen. She'll be better. She won't give him another reason to hit her.

And then he'll be safe.

From her.

12

BRIELLE

Brielle can't take it any longer!

The residual guilt from Mr. Sinclair's vision, and her own guilt at having failed Cassandra, has amplified to an intolerable level, and she *needs* to confront Cassandra about it. Brielle realizes that she's not thinking rationally. That she might expose her gift if she pursues this course.

But, at the same time, she doesn't care. This is someone's life she's dealing with. What does it matter if the one person who needs her the most learns of her powers? She just can't bear the knowledge that, if she doesn't act, Cassandra will continue to be beaten until she graduates and leaves for college. The fact that eventuality isn't far away does nothing to ease her frayed senses.

She has to confront Cassandra. Today. Now!

She waits until the end of the school day. When she knows that all of the students have gone home for the day, and Cassandra is playing lone wolf on the track field, running like her life depends on it.

Which Brielle has only just realized, maybe it does.

Maybe poor Cassandra spends so much time on extracurricular activities as a means of avoiding going home. Knowing what's waiting for her.

Brielle's heart cringes at the thought.

She walks hesitantly onto the field and immediately sees Cassandra dashing over the tarmac. The voice of wisdom inside her head pleas for her to tread carefully, but the guilt eating away at her insides overrides all coherent thought to the point she can barely hear herself breathe, which is quite impressive as each breath comes out as a huff.

Plopping onto the bleachers, she concedes she'll need to wait until Cassandra's arduous and excessive practice session is complete; she could only imagine how much more horribly this conversation would go if she interrupts.

She watches Cassandra run, and for a long moment, she lets herself be completely consumed by this girl's over-whelmingly magnetic presence. Perhaps she's just closed herself off to it all this time, but watching Cassandra now, Brielle can see the shining summer soul blazing freely inside Cassandra as she sprints. She remembers, for a moment, how brilliantly Cassandra used to shine when they were younger. How, whenever Cassandra was doing something she truly enjoyed, she'd radiate this warmth that would rival the sun, that was impossible not to infect one with joy.

At long last, Cassandra slows, then stops just after the finish line. She hunches over bent knees, panting and regaining strength. And Brielle faces the realization that her time for patient contemplation is over.

Time to shatter the ice into a million pieces.

She rises from her bench and ambles down to the field a few yards shy of where Cassandra is rehydrating.

"You were magnificent out there," Brielle says.

Cassandra jumps, turns around, then clutches her chest with her hand. "Jeez, Brielle, what the f—"

"Sorry," Brielle pleas. "I didn't mean to startle you."

"What the heck, are you stalking me now?" Cassandra demands, flipping her hair over her shoulder and taking a big swig of her water bottle. "Did Tristan tell you what a magical time we had yesterday?"

"What? No," Brielle stammers as the faintest whisper of doubt creeps into her chest. She shakes it off, realizing that this is what Cassandra is best at. "No, there are just some things that need to be addressed between us. Er, well, between—"

"Ugh!" Cassandra huffs, hanging her head to the sky. "When are you going to get that I want nothing to do with you? That the damage you did to 'us' can never be reversed?"

Brielle shakes her head. "I refuse to believe that."

Cassandra jerks her head angrily at Brielle. "Well you'd better get that through your thick skull, you conniving witch! I want nothing to do with you!"

Brielle sighs, but her conviction has her striding confidently forward. "I don't care."

Cassandra gawks at Brielle. "What?"

"I don't care that you don't want my help," Brielle continues. "Because you need it more than anyone I've ever met. I shouldn't have given up on you all those years ago. I should have seen the signs for what they really were."

The first hint of caution shades Cassandra's expression. "W-what are you talking about?"

Brielle squeezes her eyes shut, preparing for the confession she never wanted to make. "I know about your father," she blurts.

"Excuse me!?" Cassandra shrieks, her voice echoing over the empty track.

"I know, Cassandra," Brielle repeats, not backing down. "I know that what I warned you about all those years ago… came to be. I've *seen* the welts on your back…"

Cassandra stands there, stalwart for the longest time,

until finally the faintest hint of a pucker quivers across her bottom lip.

"But how?" she whispers so quietly that Brielle barely hears it over the breeze as Cassandra tugs down at the bottom of her shirt. As if that could further hide what's already hidden.

"I've known you longer than anyone," Brielle says softly. "I know *you* better than anyone. And I'm so sorry that I couldn't save you."

Cassandra somehow shrinks where she stands. Her shoulders cave in and her head slinks downward, and Brielle can't help but close in and wrap her arms around her.

"I'm so sorry," Brielle whispers into her ear.

For a moment, they're six years old again. Best friends. Sisters by choice. Huddling together against the hardships of life.

Suddenly, Cassandra pushes out her shoulders, shoving Brielle away.

"No," she spits, lips curled into a deadly growl. "I know all about your tricks, and I won't be suckered in! You hear me!"

"Tricks?" Brielle gasps, stunned. "Cassandra, I'm coming to you as a friend. I need to tell you that you don't have to face this alone. I *know*, Cassie!"

"Stop it!"

Cassandra puts her hands to her ears, and suddenly the entire field is bathed in a blinding light that could rival the sun at its brightest. A shock wave radiates out from Cassandra and thrusts Brielle backward, rattling the bleachers before Brielle's butt lands on hard concrete.

Her teeth clack together with the impact, and Brielle winces. She sits up, staring at Cassandra, open-mouthed.

Except, Cassandra is still squeezing her eyes so tightly, she didn't see what just happened.

But Brielle can never *unsee* what just happened.

Cassandra just used some unnamable force to shove her away and blanket the surrounding area in light!

And suddenly, everything clicks into place.

The Skins abducting Cassandra weeks ago.

Tristan freaking out about a possible new team member *right after* seeing Cassandra in line at Creamy Dreams.

The bond of sisterhood she's always felt toward Cassandra, even after their falling out.

With wide eyes, Brielle clambers to her feet, desperately holding onto the bleachers to support her.

"Oh my god, you're the next Zodiac Guardian!"

13

CASSANDRA

"What?" Cassandra asks, breathless as she opens her eyes and looks up at the one girl she wants, now more than ever, to get away from.

"You're one of us," Brielle whispers, eyes wide with shock. "I should have known. All this time…"

Cassandra drops her hands and regards Brielle as a torture victim would her tormentor. "What are you talking about, one of you?"

Brielle takes a step closer, and Cassandra stumbles backward.

"You're a Zodiac Guardian, Cassie," Brielle says in a steady voice, holding out a flat, palm down hand that's meant to calm.

"I—you—what?" Cassandra stammers, feeling even smaller than she does during her father's whippings.

Brielle raises sympathetic brows. "You just sent out a shockwave of pure light." Brielle looks down at Cassandra's hands. "Your hands are still glowing."

Instinctively, Cassandra balls her fists and stuffs them

behind her without a single look; she can feel that Brielle is right.

She lost control. But it's never been like that.

"We can help you," Brielle says, reaching a hand forward.

Cassandra jerks away, as if Brielle's touch might burn her. "No!" she says, her voice shaky and sharp. "I don't want your help. Stay away from me!"

Before Brielle can spout another bout of poison, Cassandra runs. The muscles that were exhausted only a second ago, seemingly unable to push any farther, now sprint like her life depends on it. She absolutely has to get as far away from Brielle as possible, as quickly as possible.

Brielle just saw undeniable proof of Cassandra's most guarded secret!

And she'll expose it to the world!

What if there are security cameras on the track field? They'd have seen it, too. She's done for! She'll be the freak she's been trying to convince the whole town Brielle is for the past ten years. The freak with the glowing hands.

She doesn't even bother with stopping at the gym to change out of her sweat-drenched clothes. She runs straight through the school, out the front door and past the parking lot. Her car could get her farther faster, but nothing will offer the same ventilation, the same catharsis, as running till her legs give out.

Zodiac Guardian.

One of us.

What does any of that even mean? Is Brielle part of some freaky cult? Cassandra wouldn't be surprised. Whatever it means, she wants nothing to do with Brielle and her black magic. She wants to be normal. She *needs* to be normal!

What will her father think?

She desperately pushes the thought away. She can't think like that right now. Can't let herself imagine the rejection waiting for her in that darkest of possibilities. One that is now closer to reality than it's ever been.

Without meaning to, she lets in the memories she's purposely blocked out. From the night of her abduction.

"Which Zodiac are you?" a masked and technologically deepened voice had asked as she was strapped to an uncomfortable chair.

"What are you talking about?" Cassandra had asked, her vision so blurred by tears of panic that she could barely make out the silhouette hovering between her and the too bright fluorescent light.

"They see something in you, or they wouldn't be following you," the voice declared. *"So, which Zodiac Heir are you?"*

"I really don't know what you're talking about," Cassandra wept.

Another surge of cripplingly painful electricity coursed through her body, tightening every muscle in agony.

It seemed to last forever, but when it finally ceased, she had cried out. *"What do you want?"*

"We want the staff, you stupid girl," said the voice mockingly, a hoarse and manipulated chuckle following. *"Tell us where it is, and we might let you live."*

Cassandra cried, wanting desperately to give these people what they wanted so she could go back home. To her father, whose punishing persona was only mildly less awful than this.

"We'll kill your family if you don't tell us," the masked figure said menacingly.

And suddenly, all fear and pain had vanished. In that moment, she didn't care if they killed her. Didn't care if they killed her family. Because, in all honesty, what was she living for? Her dad only cared enough to beat her when she messed up, and her mom didn't even care enough for that! She'd survived worse than this torture before, and, as much as she hated to admit it, she'd probably survive this, too, and be no better or worse off.

"Do what you must, but I'm of no use to you," Cassandra spat.

She'd tightened her hands, nails digging in deeper than they ever have before. No matter how much agony she was about to endure, her one win will be to keep her powers secret. She wouldn't die weak. A failure.

"Oh trust me, we'll do our absolute worst," said the masked figure as it loomed over her, a twisted note of glee in that manipulated voice.

"I can take it," Cassandra had whimpered, right before another surge tightened all her muscles in an agonizing seizure.

She must have fainted, because she can't remember a single thing after. She'd lied to Tristan, of course, when he asked what she remembered of that night. Only because it was so horrible, she wished she could just forget it. Because her father would ask too many questions. And she never believed Brielle wasn't involved. It had been Brielle and Tristan who'd saved her after all, and in the very same vicinity as Tristan's parents were murdered under mysterious circumstances.

She'd tried her best to forget, to put it behind her. But hearing Brielle mention the term "Zodiac" just now has Cassandra's mind stuck on that night like gum to a shoe.

Her legs have carried her a mile up the road, past Creamy Dreams where all her friends are laughing and enjoying a stress-free life. Oh, how she envies them. They have normal families, normal lives, normal teenage drama to deal with. She'd give anything to be the persona she portrays to them. The smart, confident, top-of-her-class girl with the world at her feet.

Nothing could be further from the truth.

She's a fraud! A freak under the surface that no amount of concealer can hide. And now Brielle knows.

An oxygen deprived cramp has her coming to a halt, and she buckles over her bent and aching legs, gulping for air.

Exaggerated and demanding pants force their way through her mouth, her chest heaving for dear life.

She can go no further.

"Cassandra?"

The voice is familiar, but not one that she truly knows. She looks up to see Jareth and an unknown brunette giving her concerned looks from their post against the wall of whatever building she stopped in front of.

"Are you okay?" Jareth asks, coming toward her like he's ready to rescue her.

"I'm fine," she says through heaving breaths, swatting his helpful hands away. But she's not fine. Nothing may ever be fine again. In fact, she truly may not be able to stand up, but even knowing that, she can't allow herself to accept his support.

"You don't look fine," says his dark haired companion, coming closer as well. "You look like shit. No offense."

Cassandra doesn't know why, but a shaky and exorbitant laugh bubbles up her throat and out her parched lips. Perhaps it's just that no one has ever told her the truth so blatantly before. So unafraid of her status. This girl clearly does not go to their school.

Perhaps it's that fearless honesty that has Cassandra finally accepting Jareth's outstretched hand and allowing him to lead her to the curb to sit. Without a word, he hands her a half-drunk bottle of water, and she takes it, greedily chugging it.

When she's finished, she wipes her mouth and hands him the empty bottle. "If you ever say a word of this to anyone, I'll end you."

Jareth chuckles, completely unoffended. "I'm sure I'll manage."

Cassandra laughs, too.

The curvy brunette plops down beside her. "You don't

have to tell me what he did to you, but just give me a name and I'll beat the crap out of him." The look in the girl's eyes is so sincere, so unapologetic, that Cassandra can't help but burst into hysterics.

She laughs so hard that she cries.

The couple waits until Cassandra's laughter subsides. They must think she's gone mad. And, honestly, maybe she has. Maybe she's finally cracked.

When she can control her motor functions once more, Cassandra shakes her head. "No, it's nothing like that." Her default smugness returns. "No guy would ever dare cross me."

The girl snickers. "Okay, then what's the deal?"

Both look at her expectantly, waiting for her explanation.

Cassandra remembers, like a punch to the gut, that Jareth is one of Brielle's inner circle. Can she trust him?

Just looking at him. The sincerity on his and his girl-friend's faces, tells her she can. Or maybe she can get a glimpse into Brielle's secret life. Would he even know about it?

"Brielle said some weird things to me just now," she cautiously admits, watching Jareth's face for a reaction.

His brows quirk, but the genuine concern hasn't wavered. "What did she say?" he asks when she doesn't elaborate.

Cassandra forces out a snort and rolls her eyes. "She told me I'm a...what was it? A...Zodiac Guardian?" She plays it off like she doesn't care, like the whole encounter meant nothing to her.

But the shadow that falls over both of their faces isn't missed by Cassandra's alert, paranoid senses.

The couple shares a glance. Then Jareth swallows and looks Cassandra in the eye. "What happened when she said that?"

Cassandra leans in, conditioned by years of jumping on

the insecurities of others. "So, you know what it means, then?"

Jareth sighs, a heavy frown creasing his surprisingly handsome features. How had she never noticed how cute he is? "I do."

Oh no. Cassandra's made a terrible error by confiding in them.

"Only, it wasn't Brielle who told me the first time," Jareth says, his voice hushed. "It was Tristan."

Cassandra's eyes nearly bug out of her head. "What?"

How severely has Brielle crippled sweet, innocent Tristan's mind?

But at the same time Cassandra questions this, she can't deny the little nagging itch in her belly that tells her she's missing something. Something terribly paramount.

Something she doesn't want to admit.

Jareth nods. "I had a hard time believing it at first, too. But..." he glances at the brunette, and the girl nods in understanding. "I soon came to learn that it was very much not a joke." He turns back to Cassandra, his dark eyes swirling with seriousness. "If Brielle told you that you're a Zodiac Guardian, it must be true."

Cassandra's head is shaking before she even realizes it. "What does that even mean? What is a Zodiac Guardian?"

"Uhhh." Jareth pauses, seeming momentarily stunned, lost. "I'm not the best person to explain that."

"Then who is?" Cassandra pushes, her curiosity suddenly demanding and unforgiving.

He leans in even closer. "Tristan."

She shakes her head, unsure if the dizziness she's feeling is from bodily fatigue or mental and emotional strain.

Suddenly, the moment with the yellow gem stone flashes in her mind.

"If you really want to know, come by the house and talk

to him," Jareth says, his eyes surprisingly clear for how dark they are. Like she can see right through to his open-book soul.

"The house?" she asks, catching the hint of shared residence in his words.

"Oh, uh, yeah." He rubs the back of his head. "I'm bunking with Tristan since the Sk—uh, since my house burnt down."

Cassandra knows there's more to that story, but she can't handle any more truths right now. She decides it's best to leave it where it is.

She regards him for a moment, feeling like this is a blue-pill-or-white-pill moment like in *The Matrix*. She's not sure she wants to go further down the rabbit hole.

But what choice does she really have? She can't just deny for the rest of her life the secret that her palms literally shine a light every time she gets upset. Especially now that she exposed it to Brielle. And what if they really do know something? What if they could help her get control, before she hurts someone again?

What does she have to lose?

"Fine," she concedes at last. "I'll see what Tristan has to say."

14

TRISTAN

Tristan paces the dirt-covered floor of the partially-built apartment building he's in. Graffiti covers the walls around him, most of it pretty harsh and ugly, some of it actually pretty good, all of it fairly faded. No one has been here for a very long time.

Which is just the way he wants it if he has to meet Jack Cadbury.

Tristan was still reeling from McNally's call when his cell had started ringing again. Seeing Jack's name on the screen hadn't helped his mood, but he'd pressed the little green phone icon, deciding to treat Jack like a Band-Aid—rip it off and tell yourself you barely felt it.

"We need to talk," Jack had growled.

"We really don't," Tristan had snapped back. "Is contacting me part of the truce?"

Jack's sigh had sounded like it was being pushed through gritted teeth. "It is now. We need to talk."

"Look, Jack, I'm kinda busy right now—"

"I want to meet as much as you do, Ayers, but right now we have a common goal."

Tristan had stilled. "I doubt that."

"I know McNally contacted you. We both want him back behind bars."

A great big curse word had flashed through Tristan's mind, and as he paces even harder, this time he mutters it out loud. Those words had him agreeing to meet Jack. Grudgingly. More like, unwillingly.

But he's still here, at an abandoned building that Google maps found him in a seedy part of New York, waiting for the FBI agent who's determined to uncover Tristan's secret. He wipes his hand down his face. A wormhole. McNally. Cassandra. Now Jack.

Tristan must've been a really bad person in a past life.

"Nice place you got here," Jack calls from the doorway.

Tristan stops mid-pace, standing in the center of the shell they're in. "I thought it was fitting considering you're determined to paint me as a criminal."

Jack enters, his gaze sweeping the room in much the same way Tristan did when he first entered. Piles of timber and metal in the back corner (no one hiding in there, Tristan checked), a doorway leading to a set of stairs (also declared clear after Tristan did a sweep), an undisturbed layer of dirt caking everything (free of any recent footprints).

"The place is clear," Tristan informs him. "We're alone."

Still, Jack checks behind him as he moves further into the room, which is exactly what Tristan would've done.

Jack stops a few feet away, unsmiling and alert. "McNally contacted you."

"So much for the truce, huh?" Jack would have to be keeping an eye on Tristan to have known this.

"Whether you want to believe it or not, I was tailing McNally when I found that out."

Tristan shrugs, knowing Jack isn't likely to tell him the

truth if it were otherwise. "If you've got a lead on McNally, then you don't need me."

"He's disappeared again," Jack growls in frustration.

Because he can turn invisible. "That's too bad."

Jack pins Tristan with a hard gaze. "You're probably his first target. What did he want?"

Tristan wants to tell Jack the truth as much as he wants to eat his own cooking, but Jack has access to resources Tristan doesn't. "Total surrender," he says, the words sharp and bitter on his tongue. "And if we don't, he'll kill me and everyone I care about."

Jack's eye twitches and Tristan wonders if he's thinking of Veronica. If he knew exactly how close his daughter is to all this, his entire face would be having a fit.

"And?"

Tristan shrugs. "He hung up. Probably wanted to give me time to think over the generous offer."

"You should take him up on it."

"Your fellow agents are right, you are crazy."

Jack doesn't even blink at the insult. "You agree to a time and place and we set a trap. I'll have enough agents and fire-power here to make sure he doesn't get away."

"No."

"This is our chance to catch the bastard, Tristan. Think it through."

Tristan shakes his head. Jack doesn't know what McNally is capable of. "We'd be sitting ducks. You're underestimating how much McNally wants us dead."

Jack jumps onto those last words like the fox he is. "Why? Why would he want you and your friends dead so bad?"

Tristan's hands clench and unclench. Maybe if he gives Jack enough of the truth, he'll be able to throw him off the scent. "There's an organization, a secret one, that has the lofty goal of world domination. If it succeeds, things won't end well for most people. My parents died trying to stop them."

Jack nods, looking unsurprised. "What's this organization's name?"

Tristan ignores the question. "It's growing in influence and they're infiltrating other organizations." He raises a brow at Jack. "Including the FBI."

Jack blinks, realizing Tristan's talking about his own boss. "I need a name—"

"That's why I suggest you honor our truce and spend less time trying to prove I'm something I'm not." Tristan angles his head. "And focus on catching McNally without using me and my friends as bait."

Jack's jaw looks like it's turning to stone, he has it clenched so tight. "I'll get McNally," he promises quietly. "But if you give me a name, I can—"

Tristan's hand shoots up to stop him. "We met, I told you what McNally said. That's as far as we go, Jack."

He stares at Tristan for long seconds, but Tristan doesn't look away. Doesn't blink. Doesn't back down. With a curt nod, Jack spins on his heel and leaves.

Once he's alone again, Tristan allows his shoulders to unwind. Jack isn't going to give up on his alien theories, but maybe this conversation will send him sniffing elsewhere. Some poor multinational company might be getting their phones tapped.

Tristan frowns. The part about Chardis being able to infiltrate organizations, including the FBI, is disturbing. Chardis got to McNally. What if he gets to Jack…

Shaking his head, Tristan decides to focus on the issues that are very real right now, not ones that he'd rather not add to his plate.

He needs to meet with the others. They need to talk about Cassandra.

Before he's taken a step, his cell rings. Every muscle clenches as he glances at the screen, wondering if McNally is calling with another offer.

But it's Jareth's name on the screen. Relieved, Tristan picks up. "Hey, please don't tell me we're eating in tonight. I need some good news for a change."

"Well, my mother always said good news is in the eyes of the beholder."

Tristan's gut clenches at the way Jareth is hedging. "It's my turn to cook, isn't it?" he quips lightly.

"I have Cassandra with me. I think we all need to sit down and have a chat."

Tristan rubs his forehead. "We're going to need some of your mother's tea, aren't we?"

"Probably."

"Okay, I'll call Brielle. I can be at the house in twenty."

Jareth hesitates. "If Brielle's going to be there—and I think she should—maybe we don't do it at the house?"

Wondering what that's about, but willing to trust Jareth on this, Tristan agrees.

He glances around at the barren, dirty space he's in. "I'll send you an address."

It's time for the next Zodiac Guardian to join their ranks.

15

BRIELLE

Brielle wasn't sure what she expected to happen after confronting Cassandra, but finding out she's the next Zodiac Guardian wasn't anywhere near her wildest imaginings.

As she bikes home, she now understands Tristan's hesitation at disclosing who he thought the next Zodiac was. She's now certain that Cassandra's his suspect, and of course he'd want to be sure before dropping that bomb on Brielle. They'd been in Creamy Dreams, and Cassandra was right behind him. How could she have overlooked the possibility that he'd seen something from her?

Because she so desperately hadn't wanted it to be true.

But that was then. When Brielle viewed Cassandra as the nastiest person on the planet. Now that she knows the truth behind Cassandra's actions, she's almost glad that Cassandra is the next Zodiac. This is their chance to heal their relationship. Brielle's chance to truly help Cassandra, using only the bond that Zodiacs have.

Only Brielle has no idea how to reach Cassandra, how to convince her that this is the path she was destined for. It might end up that Cassandra rejects her calling, only for the fact that Brielle is part of it.

As Brielle approaches her house, she notices a silver sedan sitting just outside the property line.

The sight of the vehicle has her stopping the bike a few yards behind it. She doesn't recognize it. Could it be one of Frank's work friends? If so, why isn't it parked at the house against the fence where guests usually park?

She hops off her bike and slowly pushes it up the road, pretending not to be examining the car intently. A strange feeling tickles up her spine, like that feeling you get in the dark when you feel something is about to jump out and grab you, but she shrugs it off as paranoia elicited by the past few days' events.

As she walks past the left side of the car, she sees that someone is still sitting in the driver's seat. He's a young man, a bit older than her by the looks of it, with crew-cut dark hair and glasses. She smiles curtly at him as she passes, then stops.

This doesn't feel right.

But how does she proceed?

Going on instinct, she drags her bike backward and approaches the driver's door. She raps her knuckles on the window.

The man behind the plexiglass looks up, then rolls down the window.

"Is everything okay?" she asks, playing the part of concerned citizen. "Do you need some help?"

He smiles dismissively. His face seems familiar somehow, even though she's sure she's never seen him before. "No, everything's fine," he says, waving a hand. He pulls up a phone and the screen lights the interior of the car, making her notice the stack of manilla folders piled on the passenger's seat. "I was just a bit lost for a moment, but I think I've found my way. Thanks anyway."

Then he rolls the window up and slowly drives away.

Dust builds behind the disembarking vehicle, and Brielle knows one thing.

He was lying.

She tries to memorize the license plate, but the dust is too thick to get a good look.

Damn!

She has a mind to call Tristan, but what is she going to say? Some rando was parked outside her house and claimed to be lost? Not exactly compelling evidence. And even if she sensed he was lying, that doesn't mean he's a Skin. But then...what is he? Who's he working for?

Shaking her head, she clears her mind. This day has been too much of a roller coaster for her to indulge the spiraling conspiratorial thoughts that threaten. All she wants to do is get inside and forget for a brief moment.

Brielle pushes the bike up the drive and locks it in the garage before heading inside.

"It was so nice to hear from you. I'm glad you're both doing well."

Bea hangs up the phone as Brielle enters the kitchen, and she doesn't need any super powers to tell Bea is in an emotional state.

She pretends not to have noticed. "Sorry I'm late. Got caught up with stuff after school." Simple and to the point. A vague description of what actually happened. Not a lie. No guilt required.

"Oh, that's fine, dear," Bea says, her voice distant and her expression preoccupied.

"Need help with dinner?" Brielle ventures, hoping for the distraction.

"Uh, sure," Bea says, eyes focusing on the present. "I got

swordfish steaks from the store today, thought we'd experiment."

Brielle's lip tip up in a wide smile. "I do love experiment-ing." Then she attempts an imitation of a mad-scientist laugh, but fails miserably.

Bea cracks up despite her best efforts to stop it.

They work on the fish together, Brielle starting by pretending the thick cut of fish steak is a sword and slashing through the air with it, which is welcomed by more light-hearted laughter from Bea.

"Careful, don't poke an eye out," Bea teases as they set down the steaks to season them.

Brielle jokingly covers one eye and says in her worst pirate accent, "Aye, matee!"

Bea laughs so hard she cries, and Brielle is happy she could take both of them from their worries.

Halfway through searing the steaks, Bea turns knowing motherly eyes on her.

Uh oh.

"You know, this whole thing with Cassandra," Bea begins. "I get it. That call you walked in on, that was my college bestie, Sam." She takes a deep, wavering breath, as if to prep herself for a difficult confession. "When Frank and I were having a hard time conceiving, she'd offered to be our surro-gate. I…" she squeezes her eyes shut, and Brielle can feel the guilt she harbors. "I have no eggs, so we got a donor, and Samantha carried it all the way. Well, halfway through the pregnancy, she developed feelings for the baby. She couldn't bear to let it go. I was still so hopped up on hormones from all the fertilization drugs that I broke down. She wired money directly into our accounts to compensate us for our losses, but we got into a huge fight and didn't speak since."

Brielle can feel every emotion Bea is struggling with, and she fights back the tears the trauma incites.

"After our adoption went through, I reached out to see how she was doing," Bea continues, her voice shaky. "I've always felt horrible for how everything turned out. She was my best friend, and I still don't know who was right in that situation, or if anyone was. All I knew was that there's been this hole in my heart where her presence should be. That was her on the phone. We made amends, and turns out she and young Elizabeth are doing very well. Elizabeth is just entering middle school."

Brielle can barely stand the pain she feels by osmosis for Bea. Unable to stop herself, and not wanting to, she throws her arms around Bea, wrapping her in a tight and comforting hug.

"I'm so sorry, I had no idea," Brielle barely manages to say through the stricture in her throat.

Bea pats Brielle's arm around her. "It's okay. Really. If the situation had been reversed, I don't think I could give up a child I carried either. Lord knows, I've tried to carry several."

Brielle tightens her embrace.

After a very silent and bonding moment, Bea withdraws and looks Brielle in the eye. "What I want you to take away from this is, there's no obstacle that true friendship can't conquer. If you felt the same bond I did with Sam, and I sense you do, don't give up. It's never too late to fix things."

Brielle swallows, having forgotten the pretense to this confession. Cassandra.

She shakes her head. "I actually tried today." She raises sheepish eyes to Bea. "That's why I was late. And she rejected me still."

Bea nods and pulls Brielle into a motherly hug. "I know. It's hard on both sides. Emotions are powerful things and warp our perception. But as long you hold strong to your truth, and she to hers, you'll both figure it out eventually. Just don't give up. You're still young. You both have all the time in the world."

Only we don't. Chardis's wormhole may swallow us whole and devour us completely.

Brielle pulls back and smiles. "Thanks. I'll keep trying," she says, even as she feels it won't help. Not until Cassandra is willing to open her eyes and her heart.

Bea looks at the fish steaks that are ready to go into the oven. She wipes her eyes. "Okay, I'll just pop these in the oven and we'll be good to go."

Before Brielle can say anything, her phone rings in her pocket. She pulls it out to see Tristan's name flashing in bright lights. Her heart twitterpating at the sight, she immediately answers it.

"Hey?"

"Another emergency meeting. Can you make it?" Only it's not Tristan's voice, it's Jareth's. And it sounds urgent.

Brielle looks at Bea, who's bending over the oven as she slides the pan of swordfish into its eager maw.

"Uh, I can try," she says. "Can I just skype it?"

"No, you'll want to be here for this," Jareth says. Then he whispers, "Cassandra is coming."

Like every siren in Brielle's head and physique is flashing a red alert, she automatically declares, "I'll be right there."

She hangs up and turns to Bea. "You know what we were just talking about?"

Bea turns to her, eyes filled with knowing. "Go," she says.

"Thank you!" Brielle praises with the utmost gratitude for her parents' unwavering faith, then rushes out the door.

This is her chance.

Cassandra is willing to listen!

CASSANDRA

W hen Jareth had said, "Please come by," she hadn't expected this.

The rundown apartment block—at least, Cassandra thinks that's what it is—she walks up on is so far from a supernatural meeting place, it has her spine sizzling in suspicion. The entire block is absent of any movement, save from the crickets and bats that flicker in and out of sight under the orange street lamps. There are garbage bags everywhere, as if that's the new trend in décor, and every inch of brick wall is covered in graffiti, ranging from terrible to tolerable.

What if these so-called Zodiacs really were responsible for her abduction a month ago? What if this is just some trick to get her to go some place no one would ever look for her?

But she trusts Tristan. And oddly enough, she trusts Jareth. And she's willing to believe Tristan has answers, in which case, she desperately wants to hear them.

As Cassandra cautiously approaches in the fading twilight, the forms of Jareth and his girlfriend depart from the shadows.

"Sorry," he says. "I didn't expect this locale when I invited you earlier, but Tristan thought it would be best." Even Jareth's face is tensed with anticipation.

"Best for what?" Cassandra can't help but ask.

"I guess we'll see," says his curvy brunette companion, shrugging under her over-large hoodie.

Frowning, Cassandra follows them into the unknown, half-expecting some thugs to jump out at her and accuse her of strange things like last time.

They pass through what was obviously meant to be a grand entrance doorway—but the doors have been ripped out—and into a wide expanse of dirt-covered ground where any plans of future rooms have been torn away, leaving nothing but a long, wide cavern surrounded by brick.

Tristan stands in the middle of the space, his hands in his pockets and his face pensive, dust floating around him.

He looks over his shoulder as the three of them approach. A weak smile twitches up his plump lips as he meets her questioning eyes.

"Cassandra," he says softly. "I'm glad you decided to come. This will be a big milestone, for all of us, I'm guessing."

She says nothing. What is she supposed to say? He's the one who's supposed to have the answers.

They close the distance, and he looks at his phone, his smile crooking into a weird frown. Then he looks up at her. "I invited a third party. I hope you don't mind." His expression is sheepish, and she doesn't miss his gaze flitting over her shoulders, which she follows.

Brielle has just entered the structure.

"Bye," Cassandra says instinctively, heading for the closest broken out window.

But Jareth's hand grips her forearm and she stops, even though she knows she could easily shrug out of his unassuming hold. "You need to hear this, Cassandra," he says, his expression solemn as the grave.

She rolls her eyes and crosses her arms once he lets go.

Brielle walks toward them with a reticent expression, her eyes averted, and Cassandra can see that she carries the very same box Tristan had shown her the other day.

Cassandra's curiosity is piqued. She can't deny that she wants to see the citrine again. More than that, she wants to hold it, own it! Understand why it triggered such a severe reaction in her hands.

"You came here for answers," Tristan begins, his handsome brows furrowing. "And we're hoping for some as well. Before we can tell you anything else, it's probably best if you pick up the stone."

Brielle moves in front of Cassandra, sheepishly looking up at her, holding the case open.

Cassandra bites back the anger at Brielle's proximity. "Which stone?" she asks through clenched teeth.

Tristan gives her a wry glance. "I think you know which one."

She does. It's been in the forefront of her mind since she saw it last night.

She stares at the gorgeous princess cut gem, shimmering in the box as if it's made of pure sunlight, and she can't deny the whisper that's begging her, from the very pit of her soul, to take it.

So, she does.

Her fingers close around the precious gem and she gasps, an overwhelming surge of euphoria, power, anger, relief and energy flooding her entire being. A burst of light she's no stranger to radiates out from her hand, but this time, there's no danger. The glow is warm and nurturing, and she's panting as she takes it all in. This all-encompassing sense of purpose and belonging she never thought she was allowed.

When the glow distinguishes, she stands there, tears flowing down her face as she accepts the truth. She's different. She's *special*. Everything makes sense, and even though she hasn't yet heard what these frenemies have to say, she knows it will all be true.

The joy on Tristan's face is unmistakable, and Cassandra can't help but soak up her first exposure to male encouragement.

"I knew it," he says, breathless. "From the first day I met you, I knew there was more to you than meets the eye. And then the other day, when I saw the static at Creamy Dreams, I couldn't deny it anymore."

Cassandra's breaths come in heavy pants, rocking her petite frame. "Deny what?" She needs to hear it.

"You're the next Zodiac Guardian," Tristan says, jubilant. "You're the Leo."

A wave of joy forces Cassandra to close her eyes. This is nothing like the fear she'd felt when she thought Brielle was accusing her of something earlier. This statement is an affirmation of every hope Cassandra has ever had. Even though she has no clue what it means.

"What does that mean?" she asks, her voice trembling in a way that sounds like a giggle.

Tristan waves her over to a pile of bricks that look moderately comfortable to sit on. She perches beside him, on the edge of her seat before her cheeks even touch the rubble. For the first time in her life, she doesn't care that her pants are Cartier and that they're about to get covered in filth.

He clasps his hands together and presses them to his lips before he speaks. "The Universe is divided into twelve sections, and each section has always had a Guardian endowed with certain powers to protect it. Seventeen years ago, the most powerful dark force in the Universe was somehow set free from its prison and attacked the birthing ceremony of the Gemini Heirs. I was one of them. The attack took the entire council by surprise, and every Zodiac Heir was sent to Earth for their safety. I was lucky enough for my guard, Zarius, to find me. I assume that many of the infant Heirs were sent with guards or even parents, but if they were, I've never found another.

"My entire life, Zarius raised me knowing who and what I truly am. My life's mission has been to find the other twelve Heirs and unite them into a team of Zodiac Guardians that can defeat this ultimate evil—Chardis—before he destroys everything."

"Chardis?" she says, testing the name on her tongue as her head whirls with this new information.

"As far as we know, he's a mass of dark matter that, somehow in the recesses of space and time, gained sentience," Tristan explains. "He has the power to infiltrate the minds of those he comes in contact with and possess them. More like a virus than a poltergeist or demon. We call these possessed people Skins. I've been fighting Skins most of my life. They're the ones responsible for burning down Jareth's house"—he jerks his head toward Jareth, who nods— "for killing my parents...for abducting you."

He looks down at his hands, which restlessly fumble in his lap.

"You touching that stone, making it glow like you just did," he continues, "proves that you're the fourth Zodiac Guardian. You are the Heir to the Leo stone."

"Leo," she repeats, staring down at the sunshine gem in her hands.

"It means that you can produce and manipulate photons," Tristan says. "You literally hold the power of a star in your hands, and that makes you the most formidable ally we've yet found."

The power of a star?

This is almost too good to be true!

And yet she'd known a form of his statement all her life, but never so eloquently put.

She leans forward. "So what you're saying is, I'm an alien?"

"Not just an alien, but an alien princess," Tristan says with a nod and wink.

Her heart flutters at the thought. "Okay, I'm an alien princess, and my power is…solar power? And you're an alien prince?" She juts her chin at Tristan.

He nods.

"What's your power?" she asks.

"I have the unfortunate ability of seeing the future," Tristan says with a sigh, crossing his arms. "Only, the future is never clear. I always have two visions. One that will be, and one that might be. I can never tell which vision is the true future."

Cassandra frowns. "Well, that kinda sucks. Did you foresee this?"

Tristan shakes his head.

She turns to Jareth. "What's your power?"

Without a word, he moves his hands, and floating in mid-air between them manifests a beautiful daisy, bigger than she's ever seen growing on any sidewalk. He snatches it and passes it to her. It's green, moist and fragile in her fingers, just like it had been freshly plucked from the ground.

"I'm the Capricorn. I basically have the power of imagination," Jareth says. "Anything I imagine, I can produce in real life."

A nervous chuckle escapes Cassandra's lips as she gawks at the flower. "Omigod, that's amazing!" She looks to the girl beside him. "And yours?"

The girl puts up both hands and shakes her head. "Oh no,

I'm not one of you guys. I'm just the human dating this guy." She points a finger sideways at Jareth. "Veronica, by the way."

"Hey, you absolutely are one of us," Jareth protests, sounding offended.

"Yeah, and don't sell yourself short, Veronica," Tristan interjects. "You're not 'just the human dating Jareth', you're also our very valuable FBI informant."

"What? Seriously?" Cassandra exclaims.

Veronica nods as she shrugs, her head bouncing from shoulder to shoulder. "My dad happens to be an FBI agent hell-bent on proving that aliens exist."

Wow, this all just got way more real.

The shuffling sound to her left reminds Cassandra of the other person in the space. The person who's always been a part of this, from the very beginning. Cassandra slowly looks up at Brielle.

"I suppose this means you're a Zodiac Guardian, too?" Cassandra says with admittedly too much snark, pursing her lips and arching a brow.

Brielle casts her gaze down at her feet and nods. "I'm the Libra."

Cassandra steps closer. "And?" She needs Brielle to say it, even though she's sure she already knows.

Brielle meets Cassandra's drilling gaze, her brows creasing in sympathy, which makes Cassandra's jaw clench in irritation. "I can tell when someone is lying, and sometimes, if that person's guilt is strong enough, I get a vision of what the truth is."

Triumph at being right all this time inflates Cassandra's chest. "I knew it!" She points a finger at Brielle. "I knew there was something off about you. I could never figure out how you knew the things you did."

Brielle shrugs, relief settling her features as she looks away.

That has an eerie shadow sinking through the triumph. There is something heavy being left unsaid, so heavy that it thickens the air and weighs on her shoulders. And when it suddenly hits her, Cassandra's throat squeezes shut.

Everything she thought she knew. Everything she was so certain of. She'd been too blinded by pain and anger and bitterness to allow herself to see the truth.

The realization is like a slap in the face. It's bigger than finding out that there are whole civilizations of aliens scattered throughout the Universe, bigger than learning that she's an alien princess with hands that blast photons. Bigger even than the knowledge that she's destined to fight a dark matter equivalent of the Empire. And it gives birth to new rage.

Tristan claps his hands behind her. "Well, now that introductions are out of the way, it's time for your initiation."

Cassandra turns around, putting a lid on her simmering fury for the moment, until she can address it alone. Now is not the time. "Initiation?" She juts out a hip.

Tristan smiles. "You see, you're not fully one of us until you access your suit." He flares a sexy wry brow.

"Suit?" she asks with a laugh. "What, like we're superheroes or something? I didn't realize there was a dress code. Mine better be cute, Tristan."

He chuckles, and she can hear Jareth and Veronica snickering to her left.

"I'm not actually in control of that," he says, his perfect teeth shining in the falling darkness. "Grip your stone and say the word 'Akash.'"

She narrows her eyes at him, both hesitant and excited to see what this is all about. She's going to be so pissed if this is a joke and they actually have some lame spandex costume made up for her.

Sighing, she holds up her stone, gripping it tightly, and half-heartedly repeats the gibberish word he just said.

As she stares down at her closed hand, golden rays of light peek between her fingers, the temperature of the stone increasing to a point that should be painful but is instead deliciously warm. Underneath the glow and the heat, what looks like liquid gold wraps around her hand and up her arm, and she's too amazed by what she's seeing to be alarmed.

The strange liquid climbs up and up. She watches as it closes over her chest, forming into a fashionable metallic breastplate that smartly accentuates her best bodily assets. Right in the center of her collarbone, the distinct shape of the Leo symbol carves itself out in a lighter shade of gold, and she stares at it until the shock of something coming down over her face makes her momentarily panic.

Her hands instinctively rush to her face, attempting to pull off whatever it is. But her hands hit solid metal. She sharply inhales to find that she can breathe just fine, blinks a few times to find that she can see with precision and clarity.

This is one heck of a helmet!

The whole thing is over in seconds, and she looks down to see that she is covered head-to-toe in a sleek and sexy dark gold Iron-Man-type suit of armor.

"Whoa," she says as she inspects every part of her. "This is seriously cool."

The joy and sense of freedom that flood her system are so strong and intoxicating, Cassandra feels almost dizzy. She feels like she can do anything! Face anything! She dares Chardis to come at her right now, because she's an unstoppable force!

"I hate to disappoint you, Cassandra," Veronica says. "But your suit isn't cute. It's hot!"

They both laugh. Even Brielle chuckles quietly.

Cassandra turns back to Tristan, a bright and eager smile hidden behind her helmet. "What can it do?"

"We haven't fully tested the suits yet," he replies. "But they can absorb impacts, heighten our senses and our combat skills. I'm willing to bet yours even amplifies your solar power."

"Hmm," she says, glancing around the structure. She sees a pile of garbage bags stacked in the far corner.

That'll do.

Feeling like a badass, Cassandra stretches out her hand toward it, palm out, and wills the heat that's always been waiting under the surface to release.

The blast is immediate.

Brilliant light shoots out of her palm and incinerates a perfect circle into the garbage stack. Ashes and bits of charred plastic waft down the cavity, and singed shreds of paper rain down all around.

The other four erupt with gasps, hoots and hollers as they close in around her.

Tristan pats her on the shoulder. "Holy pitch, that was amazing! Chardis won't know what hit him!"

His praise feels so good, it pushes her intoxication into euphoria.

"Do it again!" Veronica urges, whipping her head around as she searches. Then she points excitedly to a rotting pallet leaning against the opposite wall. "Blast the pallet!"

Cassandra eagerly obliges, and they all cheer as the wood explodes into fiery splinters.

This has officially become the best night of Cassandra's life!

TRISTAN

Holy pitch! Four Zodiac Guardians now stand together, in one room.

Four!

Every single cell in Tristan's body is happy dancing. What's more, embers and flakes of ash are still floating to the ground like confetti. Cassandra's powers are the most offensive they've seen, yet!

She goes to shoot another of her blasts and Tristan quickly leaps forward. "Whoa, let's not barbeque the whole joint."

He can feel her hesitate, but a moment later Cassandra drops her arm.

"Now, all you need to say is *Akash* again and the suit will retract."

There's another hesitation, but then Cassandra murmurs the word. In a flash, her suit is gone and she's left clutching the citrine, the biggest smile he's ever seen lighting up her face. "Now that's cool."

"It sure is," Tristan says, enjoying having a Zodiac who's excited to learn their true identity. "Although, don't forget who we are has to remain secret. We don't use our powers or the suits in public."

Cassandra pouts. "But I look hot."

Chuckling, Tristan winks. "What would the mighty Mr. and Mrs. Sinclair think if they saw you all decked out in an outfit like that?"

That seems to sober her. In fact, she almost seems to shrink inside herself, a stark contrast to the impressive warrior woman of only a moment ago. "They can never know."

Tristan nods, wondering if Cassandra's realizing these powers and identity come at a price. "And you also need to realize what we're up against." He turns to the others. "While we're all here, we need to talk."

That has their attention. Jareth frowns, grabbing a hold of Veronica's hand. Brielle crosses her arms so tight, Tristan has to stop himself from going to her. Cassandra, on the other hand, plants a hand on her hip as she flicks her hair over her shoulder.

Tristan levels his gaze at her, needing Cassandra to understand exactly how serious this is. "The Skins I mentioned, one infiltrated the FBI."

"He was my dad's boss," adds Veronica.

"Yeah, and he captured Veronica and trapped her and Jareth in his burning house," says Tristan. "We defeated him and he was arrested, but he recently escaped."

Cassandra frowns. "You don't kill Skins?"

"We do if we have to," Tristan says flatly. "When it's our lives or theirs."

Cassandra's hands clench reflexively and Tristan has no idea what that means. "So, this guy's looking for you? For…us?"

"McNally's mission is to kill the Zodiacs," Jareth mutters. He glances at Tristan. "Particularly the Gemini Twins."

"You have a twin?" Cassandra asks in surprise.

Something shifts uncomfortably in Tristan's gut. "More like a second Gemini, the other half of my Zodiac. When joined, we're prophesied to be the one power Chardis can't beat." He can't look at Brielle as he says the next words. "She's my soulmate."

But Cassandra's eyes fly to Brielle. "But you haven't found her yet…"

Veronica steps forward, all business. "And right now, we need to focus on staying alive long enough to find her and the other Zodiacs."

Which is why they need to talk. Tristan sighs. "McNally contacted me."

Brielle is the first to gasp. She takes a step only to stop. "What did he want?"

Tristan's mouth twists as McNally's insidious voice whispers through his mind. "Our total surrender. If we don't, he promised to kill each and every one of us."

There's silence as everyone digests this. Tristan looks to Veronica. "And your father wants to use us as bait to capture him."

Veronica's eyes widen. "What did you tell him?"

"That he can take his idea straight back on the crazy train he came in on."

Veronica winces. "He wouldn't have liked that."

Jareth's frown sinks even lower. "It's a terrible idea. McNally would be expecting it. We don't know how many Skins he's recruited. He could have an army of super strong, cold-hearted assassins waiting for us."

Brielle moves in, placing a hand on Tristan's arm. "You're not thinking about it, are you?"

The surprise at her intuitiveness takes his mind off the warm glow expanding from their one point of contact. It seems a small part of him is as crazy as Jack, because he's wondered whether they could pull it off.

Tristan shakes his head, reaching the same conclusion each time he entertained the dangerous proposition. "We're not ready."

Jareth's only just started his training, and now Cassandra needs to learn how to defend herself without incinerating the rest of them.

Brielle lets out a breath as her hand slides away. "Good, because you're right. It's far too risky."

"But it means all we can do is sit here and wait."

Jareth shrugs. "Sometimes inaction is the best form of action."

Tristan grinds his teeth. Sitting and waiting for McNally to come to them goes against his DNA.

Veronica skips closer to Jareth, squeezing his arm. "We're going to have to train more often, and for longer."

The note of anticipation in her voice is unmistakable. These two have loved the opportunity to touch and tussle. If they both weren't improving so quickly, Tristan would've said something long ago, but it seems he has to bear the pangs of jealousy every time he hears them laugh or whisper or breathlessly spur the other on.

"Yep," Tristan agrees. "Every day, if we can."

Brielle nods. "That's a good idea. It would probably be useful for you to know how to defend yourself, Cassie," Brielle says, her green gaze steady as she regards Cassandra.

Cassandra stiffens, her face suddenly carved from stone. "I've managed to look after myself perfectly well until now," she snaps. "And that was before I knew about my powers."

Tristan watches as a faint flush of pink creeps up Brielle's cheeks. Cassandra crosses her arms and looks away, but not before Tristan sees the glow in her palms. Was it Brielle's use of the nickname?

Or something else?

A harsh silence settles in the gutted building and it reminds Tristan that Brielle and Cassandra still have fractures in their friendship. He stops himself from frowning as he wonders exactly how deep those fissures are.

"I know exactly how strong you are," Brielle almost whispers.

But Cassandra still hears her. She spins on her heel. "I need to get going. I don't want my dad wondering where I've been."

She stills as if she realizes what she just said. With another glare in Brielle's direction, Cassandra stalks out the door.

Tristan turns to Brielle, conscious that they all just went from the high of discovering another Zodiac, to watching Cassandra walk away, looking like a rod has been jammed down her spine.

"We need to work as a team, more than ever," he points out, conscious of the somber note in his voice.

"I'm trying," Brielle says quietly.

The earnestness in her voice tugs at Tristan's heart. Brielle wants this conflict about as much as he does.

Surely, their Zodiac connection will only grease the wheels of healing.

He nudges her with his shoulder, pulling up a grin. "Good, because we haven't even told her about the wormhole, yet."

18

BRIELLE

Tristan's right.

If there's any hope of the Zodiac Guardians working as a team, Brielle and Cassandra *need* to make amends.

The episode at the abandoned complex was tenuous at best. Deep down, Brielle always knew Cassandra was special. Even when the blonde vixen and her popular friends were spreading rumors about Brielle being a witch, or threatening those she got close to with being made a social leper, underneath the bitterness and resentment, Brielle knew Cassandra wasn't the ordinary popular girl she claimed to be. She'd always known Cassandra had a dark side. She just didn't know with certainty from where it stemmed.

When she and Cassandra had been at the orphanage, sure, Cassandra had shown an interest in materialism, always wanted the shinier, newer gadgets. And Brielle had always sensed something menacing hiding in the shadows. A secret that refused to be unearthed, and one Brielle desperately didn't want to see.

She was always so relieved that whatever horror

Cassandra harbored never starred in her visions. She never wanted that to come between them, so she avoided any line of questioning that might cause Cassandra to lie about it. If anyone on this planet deserved privacy, it was her best friend and sister.

Even after their falling out following Cassandra's adoption, Brielle dreaded ever seeing anything from her that she wasn't supposed to.

And even now, as Brielle has seen the horrors Mr. Sinclair has dealt Cassandra over the past ten years, the sense of desperation she'd always gotten from Cassandra in the orphanage doesn't make sense. Had Cassandra done something with her solar powers even before she'd been adopted?

Brielle shakes her head as she walks up the front steps of the school. Whatever happened in the past isn't really important now. All that matters is that they mend the gaping wedge between them. The four of them can't function as a team against Chardis if two of them are at odds.

And more than that.

Brielle *needs* to make up with Cassandra. She's more certain than ever that their comradery in the orphanage wasn't just happenstance. They were *destined* to become best friends. It was only through tragedy that they ever parted ways.

Cassandra is sitting on the stone buttress at the top of the stairs, smiling and chatting with Suki and Mia, the three of them sporting tanks and work-out shorts like it isn't forty degrees outside.

Cassandra's smile turns upside down when she sees Brielle approach, which makes the other two girls turn in Brielle's direction and scowl.

"Can we talk?" Brielle asks through her suddenly dry mouth.

Cassandra regards Brielle for a moment, her glossed lips

rolling from one side of her mouth to the other as they purse in deliberation. Finally, she rolls her eyes and glances at her friends. "I'll see you guys in class."

As if following some inferred order, Suki and Mia hop off the steps and disappear inside.

Cassandra crosses her arms and arches a catty brow at Brielle. "Well, speak."

Brielle is suddenly hyper aware of the numerous students bustling around them. She nods her head toward the front wall of the building, a gesture for Cassandra to follow her down the step to a more private location.

Cassandra scoffs and kicks off the buttress to tail her.

"What is it?" Cassandra demands when Brielle finds a suitable spot and faces her. "I'm going to be seriously pissed if you make me late for class."

"Look, now that both our secrets are out in the open, we need to talk about everything," Brielle says bluntly. "We can't just keep hating each other, not if we're going to work together." She hushes her voice and leans forward. "We not only have an all powerful dark matter entity looking for us, but also a rogue-Skin-slash-ex-FBI-agent determined to kill us. You and I need to mend our differences so we can work as a team."

Cassandra drops her arms and lets out an exasperated sigh. "Okay, I get what you're saying. This stuff is bigger than both of us. And fine, I can be professional. When we're doing Zodiac business, we're on the same team. You'll have my back and I'll have yours."

The tension in Brielle's shoulders releases as she hears the very mature response she didn't expect from her bitter rival of the past decade.

Then Cassandra's eyes narrow. "But, when we're in the real world, don't expect me to act like your best friend. When we're not discussing Zodiac business, I don't want to see you or hear your voice. And I swear, if you go anywhere near my family, I'll make your life a living hell."

Brielle's chest feels as though Cassandra just sliced her open with white-hot dagger, and Brielle can't prevent the shock from making her jaw drop.

"But…why?" she manages to ask in a small voice, hurt and confusion swirling in her exposed ribcage.

She thought Cassandra understood now that she knew the truth about Brielle's power. When she'd warned her against Mr. Sinclair all those years ago, she was only trying to protect her, not to steal a family from her. She can't still be mad about that, right? Or is she mad that Brielle didn't try hard enough to save her from him?

From the corners of her eyes, Brielle sees Cassandra's palms glow before she squeezes them into fists.

The bell rings, and whatever Cassandra was gearing up to say gets wiped away by the dismissive flip of her golden hair.

"I'm not going to be late," Cassandra says, then turns around and saunters away.

But they're not finished yet, and Brielle can't let this go. She promised Tristan, and her mom, she would fix things with Cassandra. She needs to know what Cassandra's real problem with her is. She needs to understand why Cassandra still hates her after learning the truth.

And most of all, she needs to help Cassandra. She can't just sit idly by and let Mr. Sinclair continue to abuse her. That wouldn't just make her a terrible friend but a terrible human being. But she can't help Cassandra unless Cassandra is willing to accept the help.

Brielle isn't going to give up. This was only the first attempt. She's going to keep trying, at least until Cassandra tells her why she hates her so much.

19

CASSANDRA

As Cassandra sits in her last class, she feels amazing! Not only is she basically Wonder Woman, with powers stronger than any of the other three Zodiac Guardians they know of, but she's also a princess, heir to the throne of not just a planet but an entire section of the Universe!

All she has thought about the past few days since that night in New York City is movie-fueled fantasies of being a superhero and an ever-changing mental picture of what her home planet might have looked like… What her birth parents might have been like…

They must have loved her. Are they still alive? Do they think about her every day? Will she ever see them again?

And somewhere out there is an entire system of planets that adores and misses their princess.

What would her life have been like if Chardis had never attacked the Space Station seventeen years ago? If her parents had never sent her to Earth? Would she be sitting on a throne right now overhearing the troubles of her people, or dancing at a ball with elegant alien gentlemen? Would she have spent her entire life struggling to hide her powers, or would she have been encouraged to hone them and show them off at parties like parlor tricks?

Would her real parents be proud of her?

That thought, as it has the past few days, makes her daydreams darken and slip away. Despite her current family, she can't help but feel guilty for wishing she had another one. As messed up as her father is, she does love him and always strives to be good enough for him. And as distant as her mother can be, she'll never stop wanting to earn her affection.

And yet, she can't help but wonder what it would be like to not have to feel that way. To just be accepted and loved for who and what she is.

Her mind has been a battlefield of pride and joy warring with guilt, resentment and anger, and the only casualty has been her awareness in class. She had spaced on a pop quiz in math yesterday, but luckily she was able to convince the teacher to let her retake it, explaining that the upcoming track meet this afternoon had her lacking sleep. She was very relieved that her father didn't have to find out about it, and she aced it the second time around.

The final bell rings and she shakes herself out of her daydreams. She has to focus for the track meet. Her dad has an Ivy League scout coming to watch her, so she has to be on her best game.

With determination and confidence, she heads for the locker room to get ready. The meet starts in two hours, so she has to go through all of her stretches to limber up beforehand.

It takes a lot of discipline to clear her mind as she goes through her yoga positions, especially as other members of the team start filing into the locker room. They're all chatty and gossiping. None of them have the same stakes riding on this event. Most of them are only running for fun, or just to put something on their resumes because they don't want to join the marching band or soccer team.

Thirty minutes before the meet, her phone rings.

It's her father.

She takes her phone out into the hall to answer it. "Hey, Dad."

"I just wanted to remind you that the scout from Princeton will be watching you today," he says.

"Of course, I remember."

"Good, because I need you to do your best out there," he says. "Lately, you've been falling behind. Do not disappoint me this time, Cassandra."

"I won't, Daddy," she promises, throat tight. "I promise I won't let you down."

He hangs up before she can say anything else, and suddenly all the confidence that'd built up over the last few days disintegrates.

"Cassandra?"

She turns to find the last person she wants to see standing in the hall behind her.

"What do you want?" Cassandra snaps.

"I just wanted to wish you luck out there," Brielle says, ignoring the barb and offering an encouraging smile.

"Thanks, but I don't need luck," Cassandra says, tossing her hair over her shoulder, then pulling it up to tie into a ponytail.

Brielle nods, chewing on her lip. "Was that your dad?"

Cassandra scowls sideways at her with a silent warning. "Excuse me, I have a race to run." Then she turns her back on Brielle and goes back into the locker room.

When the team jogs onto the field, tremors run up Cassandra's legs, and her hands tremble at her sides. She can't let Brielle or her father slip her up. Not this time. Not when her future is on the line. If she impresses the scout, she'll be a shoe in for Princeton, or any other Ivy League school. That's her only job right now.

"Racers, to your positions," the judge announces.

Cassandra stands at her starting line beside a girl from the visiting team, and all the other runners take their places around her. She steals a glance at the audience in the bleachers. She quickly finds her father, a stern grimace on his face. Her eyes dart away, wondering which of these faces belongs to the scout, when her eyes land on Brielle.

Her jaw clenches, and she faces forward.

Breathe. Stay in control. You got this!

"On your mark," calls the judge. "Get set." The horn sounds, and Cassandra jettisons off the starting line.

She flies over the blacktop, barely feeling her feet hit the ground. The usual high kicks in, endorphins flooding her veins and giving her even more speed. She easily passes most of the runners, contending with only two others.

One lap down, and she gains advantage over the girl on the opposing team, but as they near the end of the second lap, the girl catches up and passes the other girl on Cassandra's team.

Lap after lap, the three of them play musical spaces, each of them taking the lead for a moment then losing it again.

At the final lap, desperation thuds in Cassandra's chest. She has to beat them. She has to be the first one across the finish line.

She forces speed into her already spent legs, forces air heavily in and out of her dry and aching lungs. A few more feet. Just a few more inches now.

Yes! She passed them both!

And the finish line is just ahead.

All it takes is a split second and one mis-step, and Cassandra's vision spirals down as her body falls over her tangled feet. The pavement rushes up to crash into her, skidding up the length of her forearms and scratching the skins from her knees.

Cassandra can't hear the horn blow to announce the winner, can't hear the gasps of the audience nor the fretful remarks of the runners who stopped to help her up.

All she can hear is the whooshing sound of disappointment and self-loathing that fill her ears from her rushing blood.

She allows her teammates to help her to her feet, which are now so limp they barely hold her upright. With arms fixed under her shoulders, they carry her off the field and into the locker room.

"Are you okay, Cassandra?" asks Coach Carr as she inspects Cassandra's injuries where she sits on a bench.

No. I'm far from okay.

"I'm fine," she says through gritted teeth. "Just scratches."

Coach Carr stands and puts her hands on her beefy hips. "Well, I bet your pride hurts more than anything else. But, don't worry, these things happen to the best of us."

"But not to me," Cassandra grumbles.

Coach Carr chuckles. "You'll live. During the biggest race of my career, I crashed into the girl beside me and brought down half a dozen others. It sucks now, but later you'll laugh about it."

No, I won't. I may never laugh again.

The coach cleans Cassandra's scrapes and bandages any that still bleed, mostly just her knees. When it's all said and done, Cassandra pulls on sweatpants and a jacket to cover her shame. At least the parts the world can see.

She lingers in the locker room as everyone else leaves one by one. She doesn't want to go out there. She wants to hide in here for the rest of her life. Anything to avoid facing her father. She's not sure what will be worse, the pain of his disgust at her failure, or his wrath.

"Come on, Cassandra, you can't stay in here forever," Coach Carr calls from the door she's getting ready to lock up for the day.

With a heavy sigh, Cassandra moseys out of the locker room, floating aimlessly in the hallway as the coach locks the door. Coach puts a hand on her shoulder. "It's not the end of the world, I promise."

"My dad brought an Ivy League scout," Cassandra says, deadpan.

Coach grimaces, hissing through her teeth. "Ouch."

"Yep."

With no other words of comfort, Coach pats her shoulder one last time before walking away.

Cassandra stays in the hallway for the longest time, leaning against the wall, so angry she wants to punch something but too frozen with fear to move.

Finally, she shrinks inside her hoodie and meanders slowly down the hall. She doesn't want to go home. She wants to avoid facing her father as long as she can. But she knows time won't fix this. No amount of time will make her father less angry about it. In fact, if she deliberately avoids him, that will probably only make him more furious. His beating more severe.

When Cassandra exits through the main doors, she sees Brielle perched on the buttress.

Cassandra is too overwhelmed to even scoff or roll her eyes, and she tries to walk past Brielle without acknowledgment.

But Brielle pushes in front of her, blocking her path. "Are you alright?" Her voice is pinched with concern, and for the first time, Cassandra admits to herself that the concern isn't a show. Brielle truly does care.

She angrily shrugs away the notion, not wanting any of these revelations. Why couldn't Brielle just remain the villain?

"I'm fine," Cassandra says, averting her gaze to the ground, hands firmly and safely clenched in the pockets of her jacket.

"I'm so sorry," Brielle says. "I know how much this meet meant to you. And to your father."

Cassandra's right hand leaps out of her pocket with a mind of its own and points her index finger at Brielle's face. "Don't start."

Brielle is shaken by the reaction, but she doesn't back down. "I hope you know that I was only ever looking out for you. I always hoped I was wrong about him."

"I don't want to hear it right now," Cassandra growls.

Brielle's face puckers in a sympathetic frown. "Are you afraid to go home? If you are, we can—"

"I told you, I'm not your friend!" Cassandra snaps. "And I don't care what you think you know about my father, about my life, but stay out of it!"

"I can't do that!" Brielle exclaims, pity and concern plain on her face. "I can't just sit by and watch you be treated this way! I know you're afraid, but it doesn't have to be like this. If you would just tell someone—"

Cassandra's rage has hit its boiling point.

"NO!" Cassandra shouts, shoving Brielle backward with all her force.

A flash of bright light momentarily blinds Cassandra, and when she opens her eyes again, she sees Brielle laying on the grass several yards away, her clothes smoking.

Oh no. Oh no! No, no, no!

All fury vanishes, and Cassandra rushes to Brielle's side. Both Brielle's shoulders are charred, the top half of her jacket and shirt singed completely off.

"Brielle!" Cassandra cups Brielle's unresponsive face. "Oh, please, no! I'm so sorry! Please wake up!"

But Brielle doesn't move.

Oh, God, I killed her! Cassandra screams internally, tears streaming down her face.

She wipes her cheeks and shakes Brielle's shoulders, not caring that she's touching blackened flesh. "Come on, Brielle! You're too stubborn to die!"

In desperation, she whips her head around, looking for anyone who could help. But the entire school area is empty.

Cassandra pulls out her phone and dials nine-one-one.

"What's your emergency?" answers the female voice on the line.

"There's been an accident at Mirror Point High School," Cassandra weeps into the phone. "We need an ambulance immediately!"

20

TRISTAN

Tristan places the pizza that was just delivered on the table down in HQ, his stomach growling at the tangy smell of tomato and pepperoni that wafts up through the box. "Afternoon tea is ready," he calls out.

Jareth leaves his computer, whose screen had already gone to sleep. Doesn't look like he's found much while Tristan was out.

Jareth wrinkles his nose. "I prefer it when Brielle cooks."

Tristan opens the box, ignoring the twinge in his chest. He wishes Brielle was here too, but not just for her cooking.

"You'd think having grown up without pizza, you'd be making up for lost time." Tristan arches a brow. "I got organic cheese, does that help?"

Jareth shrugs. "Not really."

"You want me to go make you something?" Tristan challenges.

Jareth's eyes widen with mock fright. He quickly picks up a slice of pizza. "This looks delicious."

Veronica appears by his side, grabbing a slice of her own. "It seems finding nothing is hungry work."

Tristan flops into a chair. "Still?"

"I can't tell if the scans I have going are tuned into the wrong channel, or if the FBI has as much as us."

Which would be zip and zilch.

Shoving some pizza into his mouth, Tristan has to stop himself from scrunching up his face at the taste. He's never getting organic cheese again.

"McNally's laying low," he mutters in frustration.

"I was so sure he'd have committed another murder by now," says Veronica. She chews thoughtfully. "It doesn't make sense."

Jareth puts his slice of pizza down. "Maybe he was bluffing when he called you, Tristan. It could've been little more than an empty threat."

"Maybe," says Tristan, not feeling very convinced. He looks to Veronica. "And nothing from your dad?"

She shakes her head, biting her lip. "I can't ask too many questions or it'll look suspicious. He seems to have bought the secret organization story, though."

Which is something. Having Jack off their backs would be one less thing to worry about.

Jareth wraps his hand around Veronica's as she fiddles with the edge of the pizza box. "We know this is hard for you."

She sighs. "I'm spying on him while he thinks I'm spying on you guys." She looks up at Jareth. "But this is important."

Lives are at stake. Far more than just those of the Zodiac Guardians.

"We just want you to know we're grateful," Jareth says quietly. "Thank you." He leans in to press a tender kiss on her lips.

Tristan's pretty sure Veronica melts. He clears his throat. "I'm just gonna go with saying thanks."

Veronica pulls away and winks at him. "I don't even need

that." She sombers. "Everyone here has had to make sacrifices."

For some reason, Brielle's beautiful face, her beseeching green eyes, floats through Tristan's mind. Losing his parents was a sacrifice he was forced to make. They're gone.

Not following his heart is also a decision that was made for him.

But Brielle's still here. Smiling. Caring.

Wishing just like he is…

Tristan shakes his head. He hasn't lost Brielle because he never had her. Plus, when he finally meets his soulmate, this will all be history.

His cell jangles in his pocket, and he grabs it, expecting to see her name on the screen. How many times has he thought of her and she called?

But Brielle's name isn't on the screen. No one's is.

Answering, Tristan yanks the cell to his ear. "McNally."

Jareth and Veronica freeze as they register who's on the phone. They lean forward, listening intently.

"Hello, Tristan," McNally purrs. "Have you considered my offer?"

"No."

"You're more of a fool that I thought," he says mildly. "I'd reconsider if I were you, especially considering you've found another Zodiac Heir."

Ice gels in Tristan's veins. "I don't know what you're talking about."

"Yes, you do. Cassandra's going to be quite a powerful Zodiac, isn't she?"

The ice spears through Tristan's chest, feeling like it just froze his heart. "What do you want, Skin?"

"Your complete surrender," McNally growls, his thin veneer of civility gone. "I'll leave Brielle, Cassandra, all of them, alone if you surrender yourself and the stones."

"You can take your offer and shove it up your soulless—"

"I thought you might say that." McNally almost sounds glad he did. "Which is why I took care of Brielle."

The line goes dead and Tristan's heart loses the ability to function.

He shoots to his feet, furiously dialing.

"Is everything okay?" Jareth asks, concerned.

"We need to find Brielle." Tristan tries to keep the desperation out of his voice but he knows he's unsuccessful. Her cell rings out so he tries again.

"Tristan?" Veronica is standing, now, too.

Brielle doesn't answer, which only feeds the panic. Tristan tries Cassandra's phone next.

"McNally says he's got to Brielle," he chokes out.

Please, no.

Veronica gasps. "What? How?"

Cassandra's phone rings out, too, and Tristan almost crushes his own cell in frustration. Brielle would answer hers if she could. She promised.

Which means there's a reason she can't.

He goes from standing to running in a blink, shooting for the stairs.

"Tristan!" Jareth calls. "Where are you going?"

"You guys see if you can track her down," he calls over his shoulder. "I'm going looking for her."

"But how are you going to—"

Tristan doesn't hear the rest of the question, but it doesn't matter. Not only does he not have time, but he also doesn't know how to answer.

He has no idea how he's going to find Brielle.

But he will.

He's not willing to consider a scenario where he doesn't.

JACK

16:26

"Did you get it," Jack asks tensely.

Clara types rapidly on the computer resting on her lap. She frowns, her eyes narrowing as she stares at the screen. Jack pulls the car over, fingers drumming on the steering wheel.

It would be nice to have a destination for a change, rather than doing aimless laps of the city in the hope they stumble on a clue.

He's hoping the call they just tapped would give them one of those.

Clara looks at him in triumph. "Got him."

Jack thumps the wheel. "Yes!" He puts the car into gear. "Where?"

Clara types again, her gaze intent on the laptop. "City outskirts. Head west. Looks like an abandoned building."

Jack has to stop himself from jamming his foot on the gas. By tapping Tristan's phone they were able to listen to McNally's call.

And they spoke long enough for them to triangulate McNally's location.

The sooner they get that murderer off the streets, the better. Then Jack can focus on the rest of what was said in that phone conversation…

Clara turns to him, and he half expects she'll suggest they call this in, ask for some backup. Jack has no intention of doing that, but he scrabbles to think of how he's going to explain that.

"What do you think they meant by Zodiac Heirs?" she asks, her head angled as she watches him closely.

Dammit. She noticed that, too. Jack shrugs like that wasn't the biggest break he's had since he started investigating Tristan. "No idea. They must be into astrology or something."

"Come on, Jack. I asked to be partnered with you because I heard you were a great investigator. Catching the Triple Murderer only confirmed that."

Focusing on taking a corner, Jack mulls over that. Clara knows there's more to the Zodiacs info than he's trying to make out.

Clara asked to be his partner because she thinks he's a good agent…

He glances at her. "I'm not sure what it means. And I'm not taking any guesses, yet."

Clara leans a little toward him. "We need to find out, Jack," she breathes.

Suddenly conscious of their close confines, Jack snaps his head back to the road. "That's the plan," he mutters.

"Down there," Clara points to an empty street on their right.

Jack's gaze flickers over the empty parking lots and decrepit buildings. This isolated corner of New York looks like just the place someone like McNally would choose to hide out in.

"That's it." Clara indicates toward what looks like a half-built apartment building.

"Looks like someone realized what a bad investment decision they'd made. No one was going to want to live here," Jack observes. He parks the car across the street and they climb out.

Taking his gun out of his holster, he notes that Clara does the same. Neither of them are taking any chances.

Ears pricked and eyes darting, Jack makes his way toward the building, Clara right behind him. The windows are boarded up so there's no way of telling whether there's someone inside.

Coming around the front, Jack sees there's a doorway with no door. He waits, listening hard.

Nothing.

With a flicker of his finger, he indicates he's going in. Clara nods, her face tight.

Stepping through the doorway, Jack quickly sweeps his gun left then right. He finds himself in a gutted-out space, little more than a pile of burned wood in the back corner.

Clara joins him, her gun doing her own arc around the room.

"Looks empty," Jack mutters quietly.

But he learned long ago that looks can be deceiving.

A quick glance down and he sees footprints in the dust. Several of them.

"Others have been here," he tells Clara.

Possibly McNally.

Keeping his hand and gun steady as his heart rate picks up, Jack walks slowly forward.

He narrows his gaze at the pile of burned timber. There's no one there, but was that an eddy of dust? He flicks his gaze toward Clara, indicating with his head that he's going to investigate.

A few more steps and Jack's gut tingles and he knows it's not the ulcer. He scans the singed wood, trying to figure out why his senses have switched gears into high alert.

It's like there's a shadow that shouldn't be there.

"Hey, you! Stop!"

Jack spins around to see Clara running to the door. A blur of movement shoots past the opening.

He breaks into a sprint after her. "This is the police!"

Outside, Clara is already rounding the corner as she pursues their suspect. Jack races after her, trying to catch sight of their target.

He takes a sharp right, stopping when he sees a teen scrabbling over a brick wall, Clara a few feet behind him.

"Stand down, Agent!" he puffs through frustrated breaths. "It's not our suspect."

The scared kid wasn't McNally.

Clara tucks her gun back into her holster in short, sharp movements. "Dammit."

Jack waits for her to join him before turning back to the front entrance. "Probably some kids, squatting."

"Sorry," she mutters. "I thought he was our guy."

"You did good," Jack assures her even as he wants to grind his teeth. He silently points out to himself it's not like there was anyone inside the building. Even if McNally was here, he's long gone now. "You saw a suspect and you followed through on him."

Clara moves a little closer. "Thanks, Jack."

Clearing his throat, Jack holsters his gun. "We'll get the bastard."

"I know we will." She smiles, her eyes twinkling.

When his cell rings, Jack's almost relieved. He steps away from whatever was just happening, glancing at the screen. "Sorry, it's my daughter," he tells Clara.

"I'll wait by the car," she offers with another smile. She turns, and Jack has to make a concerted effort not to notice the way her hips sway as she walks away.

He lifts the phone to his ear. "Hey, KitKat."

"Hey, Dad," Veronica responds. "I just wanted to check whether there's any news."

Jack glances at his cell, still not sure how he feels about Veronica being so proactive about finding out what she can.

"No," he grinds out. "We thought we had a location on McNally but it turned out to be a dud."

"Where?"

Jack glances around him. This is the last place he'd want his daughter to be. "Nowhere you need to know about."

"But, maybe if you gave me an address I could do a little hunting on the internet—"

"Actually," Jack quickly cuts her off. He has no intention of telling Veronica where he is. "I need you to find out what you can about Zodiac Heirs or Guardians."

There's a pause. "I've never heard Tristan or the others use those terms."

"I doubt you would've," Jack assures, conscious of the tension in his daughter's voice. "But this is their big secret. I can feel it."

Another pause. "I'll see what I can find out."

"Okay, but stay safe."

And trawling the internet is exactly that.

"I will, Dad. Love you."

She hangs up and Jack glances at the building.

McNally may have escaped him, but he's one step closer to catching Tristan.

21

CASSANDRA

"Can you tell me again what happened?"

A young and handsome police officer stands a few feet away from where Cassandra sits in the hospital room by Brielle's bed. He has a notepad in his hands and a quizzical look on his face.

Cassandra wipes at her nose with a tissue, her eyes stinging from all the crying she's done in the last hour. "I already told you." She sniffs. "We were working on a science experiment for a class project and it backfired."

"What exactly was the experiment?" he probes further.

"It was a model rocket," she lies with all the exasperation she's honed in her many years as a popular girl. "We must have measured the jet fuel wrong. I never thought something like this would happen." She looks down at Brielle beside her, and her face scrunches up with fresh tears, *real* tears.

Brielle's shoulders and chest are tightly wrapped in gauze, making her look part mummy, and a breathing mask is over her unconscious face as all sorts of tubes and wires string up from her body like a twisted marionette.

"Thank you for your service, officer," says the African-

American nurse as she goes straight to the vitals monitor without looking at him. "But these girls need some rest. They've both been through enough for one day."

His face looking chastised and uncertain for a moment, he puts his pen and pad into his breast pocket and nods. "Alright. But please let me know when Ms. Pierce wakes up so that I can get her statement as well."

"Uh-huh." The sassy nurse waves her hand at him dismissively, and again he looks like a lost puppy for a minute or two before resigning to leave the room.

Once he's gone, the nurse looks at Cassandra and winks.

"Thank you," Cassandra says sincerely, then glances at the nurse's name tag, "Nurse Sharon."

"Any time, hon," she replies with a warm smile. "I know how hard this must be for you. Are you two close?"

Cassandra looks at Brielle's face, and her throat tightens. "She's my best friend," she squeaks out.

"Oh, honey," Nurse Sharon coos as she rushes around to the other side of the bed to drape comforting arms over Cassandra's shoulders. "She's going to be okay. She'll just have a few scars."

Scars that cover her shoulders, that she'll wear the rest of her life.

"Have you been able to reach her parents yet?" Cassandra manages to ask.

Nurse Sharon withdraws. "Yes, and they're both on their way."

That knowledge both comforts and terrifies Cassandra. She's happy Brielle has parents who love her so much, and she doesn't know how she's going to face them knowing this was her doing. Knowing that she scarred their daughter for life and almost killed her.

Cassandra nods, and Nurse Sharon pats her shoulder.

"Can I get you anything from the cafeteria? They make a

mean Philly cheesesteak." Nurse Sharon smiles, and her ebony ringlets bounce around her face.

"No thanks." Cassandra shakes her head. "I can't eat right now."

"Alright, well, if you need anything, just push the little blue button on the remote."

Nurse Sharon leaves the room, and Cassandra is alone with Brielle for the first time since they arrived. Her phone buzzes in her pocket, but she doesn't bother to check it. Whoever it is and whatever they want is definitely not more important than this. Especially not if it's her father telling her to come home, which she's almost certain it is.

She shakily reaches over and puts her hand on top of Brielle's, gently at first, then wraps her fingers underneath.

"I'm so sorry, Brielle," Cassandra sobs softly.

Brielle was only trying to help. That's all Brielle had ever done, and Cassandra refused to see it that way. And because of Cassandra's ignorance and misplaced anger, Brielle almost died.

What if the blast had been stronger and burned right through Brielle like it did through the garbage bags the other night? The mental image is gruesome and horrifying, but Cassandra can't shake free of it. She sees it in complete gory detail, and it makes her want to throw up.

That's two near casualties now. Two innocent people she's hurt by accident with her power. She really is the disappointment her father says she is, and he doesn't even know the half of it. She hangs her head, letting hot tears drip onto her legs and soak into her sweatpants.

"Ca...san...dra?"

The sound is weak and raspy, and for a moment, Cassandra thinks she imagined it. She looks up at Brielle's face to see her beautiful green eyes shining at her under heavy eyelids at half-mast.

"I'm here!" Cassandra says, leaning forward. "I'm so, so sorry I hurt you. I didn't mean to."

"I know," Brielle says hoarsely. Her free hand slowly raises to her head and she taps her temple with her index finger. "I'd know if you were lying, remember?" Her lips tip up beneath the breathing mask.

Brielle's lighthearted response takes so much weight off Cassandra's heart that nervous laughter bubbles up her throat before it's interrupted by a sniffle.

Then Cassandra frowns, serious again. "Does it hurt very much?"

"A little," Brielle croaks.

Cassandra raises a brow. "Now who's lying?"

Brielle tries to chuckle but chokes.

Cassandra squeezes the hand she's still holding. "It's okay, you don't have to talk. Just listen, because I have a lot to say."

Brielle blinks in place of a nod.

"I've been so wrong about you all this time," Cassandra begins. "When you told me about my parents back then, I truly thought you were just trying to ruin my adoption. I went home with them, and everything was great, for a little while. Then when your accusations started to become a reality, I got it in my head that you were somehow responsible. I believed the things the other orphans always said about you, that you were a witch, and I let myself believe that you cursed me and my parents."

"Cassie," Brielle says, but Cassandra places a finger on the edge of the breathing mask and shakes her head.

"Wait, there's more. I wanted someone to blame for the way my supposed happily-ever-after turned out," she continues. "And I wanted so much to love my family, for them to love me, that I put the blame in all the wrong places—on you, and me. Even after I realized the other night that you weren't the villain of this story, that you weren't the reason my dad is…the way he is, I still needed to hate you. I was so angry that you got the perfect family and I didn't, that all those years ago you had been right all along. Part of me hated you for knowing the truth and not saving me from it when you had the chance, for not trying harder to convince me. And another part of me was so afraid that you were going to tell someone about my dad and take away the only family I've got."

Cassandra grits her teeth and closes her eyes. "I was so wrong. None of this has ever been your fault. You really are a good person. Maybe the best person I know." She chokes out a sob.

Brielle squeezes Cassandra's hand, and something strange happens. All the dark guilt that's been consuming Cassandra from the inside out like a parasite feels as though it's being sucked through their clasped hands. She can feel it move, feel the cool relief in every inch as it passes. And when it's finally gone, she feels almost blissful.

"I forgive you, Cassie," Brielle says, her voice sounding slightly less dry, and one hundred percent sincere.

Overcome with joy, Cassandra forgets herself and leans down to hug Brielle.

"Ah!" Brielle shrieks, tensing under Cassandra's hands.

Cassandra rapidly releases Brielle and backs away. "Sorry! So sorry!"

"Okay, maybe it does hurt," Brielle hisses through clenched teeth, then both girls laugh.

She closes her eyes, and Cassandra can see Brielle slowly untense and relax back into the hospital bed.

"You were wrong about one thing," Brielle says. "Your parents aren't the only family you've got." She reaches up to touch the citrine that hangs from Cassandra's neck by a dainty gold chain. "You have us. You have me. Sisters for life, remember?"

Cassandra's eyes well with tears again. "You really mean that?"

"With all my heart," Brielle vows.

Cassandra's chest swells with a powerful and unfamiliar emotion. It warms her and immediately goes to work healing the fractures in her heart. Feeling it now, she's certain she's never truly felt it before.

Love.

"Brielle?"

"Omigod! What happened?"

Both Cassandra and Brielle turn to the door to see Brielle's parents rushing in. Cassandra lets go of Brielle's hand and stands so that Mrs. Pierce can take her seat. She motions toward the door, deciding it best to give them some privacy.

"No, Cassie, stay," Brielle's voice barely carries over the concerned coos of her parents, but it rings in Cassandra's ear like a bell.

Those three words somehow warm Cassandra's heart even more, and she happily roots herself to the spot.

"Omigod, look at all this!" Mrs. Pierce frets, gawking at all the bandages.

"What happened, sweetheart?" Mr. Pierce asks, stress kicking his voice up an octave.

Brielle shoots Cassandra a look that says, "help me."

Cassandra steps forward. "We were working on a science project together. A model rocket. But I incorrectly calculated the fluids we were using. This is all my fault, and I'm so sorry." She looks both of them in the eyes as she says the last part, hoping to convey how much she means it.

The Pierces look down at Brielle.

"Well, at least you're still here," Mr. Pierce says, gently brushing his hand over the top of Brielle's head.

Nurse Sharon returns and tells Brielle and her parents

about the procedure and that she'll have to stay in the hospital for at least another day so they can monitor how she heals. Then she pulls in a cart full of food for everyone.

When the nurse gives Brielle the okay to take off the breathing mask, the stressful mood of the room begins to wane, and they all eat and start to talk.

Cassandra is amazed at how natural it feels to be like this with Brielle. Being enemies had always felt forced and difficult, like a chore she felt she had to do. And it had always been exhausting. But sitting at the foot of the bed, chatting and laughing? It's so easy, so effortless. It's like they never stopped being friends.

Cassandra hates that she hurt Brielle so badly, but she's grateful for the good that came out of it.

Brielle's her friend once more, and she's determined to never turn her back on their bond again.

22

TRISTAN

Tristan hangs up the phone, telling himself he won't call Brielle again. Each time she doesn't answer only escalates the panic. And the one thing he needs right now is a cool head.

He roars out of the school parking lot, tires squealing. The school was empty, as he'd expect it to be this late in the afternoon. But he was hoping that maybe Brielle and Cassandra had stayed back to study or something. The school library is notorious for poor reception.

But she wasn't there.

She wasn't at home.

Or at Creamy Dreams.

Or the town library.

Pressing redial, Tristan promptly breaks his own promise to himself. No answer.

"Dammit, Brielle," he growls. "Where are you?"

His heart tugs him north, and he follows his instincts. It's all he has left.

Except he quickly realizes where they're taking him. The

pale multistory building that's Mirror Point Hospital looms ahead.

"No…"

Was it his gut that brought him here? Or his dread that McNally was telling the truth?

His cell rings, jolting Tristan's pulse. Disappointment washes through him when he sees Veronica's name on the screen, even as he tells himself she wouldn't be calling him if she didn't have info.

"Have you found her?"

"No. Next best thing, though. I know where McNally is."

Tristan pulls over, his mind shifting gears. McNally's location could be Brielle's location. "Where?"

"Dad tracked him down, so I traced Dad's location using Find My Phone," Veronica explains. "He's at the abandoned apartment block we were at."

"Good job." Tristan's already turning his truck around. How did McNally know the Zodiacs were there? His breath hitches. If McNally's been following them all along, then he wasn't lying about Brielle. "I'm on my way."

"Don't do anything until we're there," Jareth shouts in the background.

But Tristan hangs up before they can say any more. His hands tighten around the steering wheel as cold, hard determination replaces the jittery panic.

McNally said he hurt Brielle.

Those will be some of the last words he ever says.

Evening is beginning to encase the apartment block as Tristan arrives. He turns his cell to silent and tucks it into his back pocket. He doesn't want anything or anyone disturbing him.

Not until McNally is dead.

Tristan approaches the building carefully. There's no hint of movement in the twilight and he hopes that doesn't mean Jack scared McNally off.

His hands clench and unclench compulsively as he moves to the entrance, but no one's there to greet him. Stepping over the threshold, Tristan sees Jack's footprints. Eyes narrowing, he notes that Jack had someone with him. Looks like Agent Cadbury has a partner.

They didn't get far, though—it looks like Jack was on his way to investigate Cassandra's little experiment—before they left again.

Still walking, Tristan looks around. Just as he expected, it appears empty. McNally is too much of a coward to show himself.

Tristan stands in the center of the room, unmoving, as he listens intently. He filters out the chirping of the crickets as night descends. The distant hum of traffic. The breeze squeezing through the gaps of the boarded up windows.

There. Barely perceptible breathing.

He smells it next. Not it, him.

The slight tang of sweat. Stale breath.

Someone else is in here with him.

Tristan angles his head, knowing this would be a whole lot easier with his suit but not willing to say the word that would deploy it. Despite their isolated location, it's too much of a risk. If someone were to see him, their secret would be out.

And wouldn't Jack like that…

Suddenly, there's the scuffling of footsteps. McNally's voice comes a few feet to the left of where Tristan located him. "I didn't expect you to surrender so quickly. I'm almost disappointed."

"Where's Brielle?" Tristan bites out.

The low chuckle is another few feet to the left. "So, it's the Libra who had you moving so fast." There's a pause and the voice moves again. "What would your soulmate think of that, Gemini?"

"You can tell me now, or you can tell me just before you take your last breath."

A gust of wind shoots past Tristan, making him spin around. This time, McNally speaks from the opposite side of the room. "Unlike the others, you're hard to trace, Tristan. You can fight without using your powers."

Tristan narrows his eyes. "You can track us when we use them." That's how the Skins found Jareth at his parents' memorial.

Why McNally's here after Cassandra tested out her powers.

"Chardis is very sensitive to any changes in dark matter," he says smugly.

"Good thing I found you, then."

"Yes, fortuitous, isn't it?"

Tristan hears the movement this time—he's ready for it. Except he's not ready for the fist that ploughs into his solar plexus. His body wants to fold in half as pain explodes, but he ignores it. McNally's playing games, and he's not going to afford him any more pleasure than he's already getting.

"Did you bring the stones?" McNally half-shouts from several feet away.

"Hell, no. Why the pitch would I do that?"

McNally growls in frustration, allowing Tristan to locate him. He counts. One. Two. Then lashes out with a strike of his own. He connects with McNally's chest but the spurt of elation is short lived as a fist painfully connects with Tristan's cheekbone. He lashes out again but finds nothing except air. McNally's gone again.

Tristan spins around. "Show yourself, you coward."

The chuckle comes from his right. "And lose the advantage? Where's the fun in that?"

Another *whoosh* of movement and Tristan braces himself. He ducks as he throws out a kick. McNally grunts as his strike misses, then grunts again as Tristan's leg connects with his thigh.

The next thing Tristan knows, he's reeling backward as something collides with his other cheekbone. Pain explodes through his skull as he collapses to the ground.

An instant later, he's pushing himself upright as he gets his bearings, using the pain to fuel his determination. He can hear McNally's harsh breathing over by the corner. That's good, it makes him easier to find.

"Do you surrender, Gemini?"

"Not in this lifetime." Tristan turns to where McNally must be standing. "Or the next, for that matter."

"Very well."

McNally doesn't even bother trying to hide his approach. Tristan waits for the space of breath, then throws the small handful of dirt he grabbed when McNally knocked him down. The pale dust hits the Skin on the chest and sticks there.

Bingo.

Tristan now has a target.

He spins around, following McNally's trajectory to the other side of the room. Tristan grins as he watches him appear. McNally straightens, adjusting his cuffs. He looks like he has no intention of running at him again, but that's fine by Tristan. He's more than happy to go to him.

It's time to finish this.

But his grin flatlines only a second later. McNally reaches into his jacket, drawing out a handgun. It's McNally's turn to smile as his finger tightens on the trigger. "I'm still one step ahead, Zodiac scum."

Tristan stands very still as he weighs up his options. He can't reach McNally before the bullet reaches him. If he runs the other way, the bullet will just end up in his back.

Dammit, he has no choice.

Tristan grips his stone, whispering the word "Akash" a split second before McNally pulls the trigger.

Everything seems too slow and too fast, all at the same time. The suit explodes over Tristan as he braces himself, not knowing if he left it too late. McNally runs at him, realizing what Tristan's trying to do.

The bullet *tings* as it glances off Tristan's armored chest. He barely feels it. McNally ploughs into him a second later.

But Tristan is now encased in his suit. He's protected. He's stronger.

And he's angry.

Tristan rams his fist into McNally's jaw and the blow rockets him backward. McNally shakes his head, trying to recover, but Tristan's already there. He aims a punch to the gut and as McNally doubles over. He deals another one to his chin.

This time, McNally is speared backward and he slides through the dust on the bare floor. He scrambles to his feet, only to find suit-clad Tristan before him again.

He raises his hands, palm outward. "Keep me alive and I'll share everything I know."

It's possible McNally's telling the truth, maybe for the first time ever, but it's too big a risk. Not when he's already hurt one Zodiac... Tristan winds up for another punch.

"The wormhole!" McNally gasps desperately. "It will open soon. Chardis is closer than you realize."

"Tell me something I don't know," Tristan mutters. "Where's Brielle? What did you do to her?"

McNally's eyes widen, fear flashing in their depths. "I lied. I never touched her!"

Slam. Tristan deals a fast punch to the nose. McNally clutches his face as blood gushes down his chin.

"Where is she?" Tristan roars as he shoves McNally back.

"In hospital, she—"

The uppercut that Tristan deals McNally has him lifting high up in the air, arcing, sailing backward. He lands with a *crash* on the pile of timbers that Cassandra half-incinerated, one of the lengths punching through his chest.

Panting, Tristan runs forward only to stop. McNally's eyes are glassy as blood blossoms from the shard of wood protruding like a jagged spear.

Tristan whispers the word and his suit disappears. The gutted room suddenly feels muted. Darker. Cavernous.

McNally's dead. And although the knowledge doesn't bring the sense of satisfaction Tristan was expecting, it does bring relief.

His cell vibrates and he answers it without even glancing at the screen.

Veronica's voice jolts into his ear. "I found Brielle."

Tristan's heart goes from thumping to frozen. "Where?"

"She's been admitted to Mirror Point Hospital."

23

BRIELLE

"Where is she?"

The sound of Tristan's frazzled voice coming up the hallway is unmistakable, and it sends Brielle's heartbeat into a hummingbird pace.

A second later, Tristan comes barging into the room with Jareth close behind. His eyes find hers in an instant and lock on, swirling with uncertainty at whether to be relieved or more concerned.

The sight of him fills her with joy, and she instinctively motions toward him, needing to hug him, to touch him, but the searing pain in her chest at the movements puts an immediate stop to that. It's also a reminder that she's permanently scarred. Will he even find her pretty now? Or will any desire he still harbors for her be forever extinguished, freeing him to search for his Gemini princess?

The thought doesn't even have time to grow roots as Tristan rushes to her and quickly but gently scoops her into an embrace. She flinches, expecting the contact of their chests to sting, but instead, it radiates a soothing warmth through her torso, and she grips his shirt as she savors the moment.

"Are you insane?" Frank shouts at Tristan, jumping out of his chair on the other side of her bed. "Let her go! You'll hurt her!"

Tristan doesn't even seem to hear Frank. He just keeps whispering into her ear, "I'm so glad you're safe," as he holds her.

"No, Dad, it's okay," Brielle reassures Frank before he can grab Tristan. "He's not hurting me. Really." *In fact, nothing could feel better.*

But she taps Tristan's back nonetheless as a gesture for him to withdraw. She loves Frank, and she greatly appreciates his protectiveness of her, but she doesn't need him to pick a fight with her best friend over her hospital bed.

Tristan releases her and lowers her softly back down onto her propped-up pillow, but he doesn't pull back further than a handful of inches, and she relishes the closeness.

"What happened?" he asks, both of his hands holding one of hers. His summer eyes are dark with intensity as they hold her gaze, and she almost forgets that they aren't the only two people in the room, that Frank, Bea, Cassandra, Veronica and Jareth are watching them intently.

Brielle knows she can't tell him the truth with Frank and Bea listening, but her stomach clenches at the thought of repeating Cassandra's lie. Her eyes dart over to Cassandra as she carefully gathers her words.

"Cassandra and I had an accident," Brielle says, widening her eyes as she speaks to convey the truth she can't voice.

Tristan looks down at her bandaged chest, and the narrowing of his eyes tells Brielle that he got the message loud and clear. He turns those narrowed eyes on Cassandra, and his grip on Brielle's hand tightens dangerously.

"You could have killed her," he growls at Cassandra, and

the girl who usually carries herself with the strength and ferocity of a lioness flinches like a frightened kitten at his words.

She looks away, her eyes downcast, rubbing her left arm with her right hand. "I know."

"Hey, this wasn't anyone's fault," Bea interjects, reaching over to put her hand on top of Tristan's, which are still clutching one of Brielle's. "Like Brielle said, it was an accident. Cassandra feels bad enough already."

Tristan looks at Bea, and his eyelids relax around those cool blue irises. But Brielle can still feel the tension in his fingers around hers, still sense his animosity toward Cassandra.

How ironic. For once Brielle is defensive of Cassandra, and Tristan is the one at odds with her.

Tristan returns his determined gaze to Brielle, and he softens even further. "Are you going to be okay? Was anything…damaged or punctured?"

She shakes her head. "No, none of my internal organs were damaged. I just have burns on my chest and shoulders that will take a while to heal." She blushes at the confession. She hasn't seen the extent of her burns, but she knows that at least the tops of her breasts were hit. It might be vain, but the knowledge that this injury has forever blemished the most feminine part of her body hurts in a way that's far more than physical.

"I'm so sorry," he says, hanging his head.

A knocking on the doorframe has everyone turning their heads in that direction. Nurse Sharon peeks her head through the doorway, her curtain of ebony ringlets spilling forward over her shoulders.

"Mr. and Mrs. Pierce, can I borrow you both for a moment to go over some insurance papers?" She winks at Brielle as Frank and Bea stand up and gather their things, as if she knew Brielle wanted some private time with her friends.

"Will you be alright here without us for a moment?" Frank asks Brielle.

"I'll be fine, Dad," she reassures him with an almost amused, long-suffering tone.

He nods and finally leaves, following Bea and Nurse Shannon out of the room.

Jareth closes the door behind him, giving them even more privacy.

And giving Tristan the red light to vent his anger.

He lets go of Brielle's hand and stands, turning on Cassandra. "Do you have any idea how much worse this could have been?" The words come out like a hiss, laced with venom.

"Yes, I do," Cassandra replies, averting her eyes and crossing her arms. Brielle can see the shame splashing red high on her cheeks

"I don't think you do." Tristan stalks closer to her. "You are the most powerful among us, and from what I can see, the most childish."

Cassandra's jaw drops like he just slapped her in the face.

"What are you even doing here? It's your foolish hatred of Brielle that nearly got her killed—"

"I know!" Cassandra shouts. "And I hate myself for it!"

Tristan fumes in place as he stares at Cassandra, whose eyes are misting but refusing to spill.

It pains Brielle to see Cassandra like this now that the two of them are back to being the friends they used to be. It was almost worth getting a little barbequed if that's what it took.

Brielle already knows how sorry Cassandra is about what happened. She can taste the guilt in the air, and it's foul. She's already alleviated it once, and she suspects she'll have to do it many more times to come, especially if Tristan keeps grilling Cassandra.

"Tristan," Brielle implores, reaching a hand out in his direction. "Can we please let this go? Cassandra and I have already made peace."

That makes Tristan look at her with wide eyes, then back at Cassandra, who nods sheepishly.

"I think what this proves is that we need to get Cassandra into training as soon as possible," Brielle continues. "Teach her how to control her powers, and how to properly use them when we need them."

Tristan grits his teeth, his fingers flexing in and out of a fist. "Alright. But no more petty arguments," he says, pointing a firm finger at Cassandra. "Nothing like this can ever happen again."

"It won't," Cassandra says with conviction.

The room is quiet for a moment, and Tristan slowly returns to Brielle's side and sits in the chair.

"McNally is no longer a problem," he says.

A chorus of surprised "whats" follows, each face wearing a different mixture of shock, relief and curiosity.

"I found him at the abandoned apartment," Tristan explains. "We fought, and I won."

"You went alone?" Brielle accuses, imagining the epic fight it must have been, and also how easily it could have gone wrong for Tristan.

"I had to," Tristan explains, face stony. "Jareth and Veronica were out searching for you. McNally called and said that he 'took care of you', so we went looking. Then Veronica told me she pinged him at the apartment. I wasn't going to let him hurt you." The emotion in his last words makes Brielle's breath hitch.

Even if she and Tristan aren't what she wishes they were,

she's very lucky to have him in her life. He really does care about her.

She looks into his eyes, and they say so many things. All the words she wishes she could actually hear but knows she never will.

"Hey Jare, I think I need some coffee," Veronica says. "Come with me?"

"Huh?" Jareth asks.

Veronica widens her already large eyes and darts them back and forth between where Brielle and Tristan are and the door. "Come with me to get coffee," she says each word with emphasis and nods her head insinuatingly toward the door.

"Oh, right. Sure," Jareth says when he finally gets the hint.

"I'll come, too," Cassandra says.

And without any further show, the three leave Tristan and Brielle alone in her room.

Tristan continues to hold Brielle's gaze for a long time, and there's no place she would rather be. She could stare into his summer eyes forever.

"I'm so sorry I wasn't there," he says, finally breaking eye contact to look down at her hand and hold it again.

"There was nothing you could have done," Brielle says, savoring the sensation of his thumb rubbing the back of her hand. "Cassandra and I had things we needed to work out. She also has some very deep issues of her own. I pushed too hard to help, and her emotions got the better of her. It's not her fault."

Tristan shakes his head, gritting his teeth. "All day, I was worried about McNally taking you away from me. Little did I know that the true threat was in our own circle."

"She's not a threat," Brielle insists. "Her accidentally hurting me was the thing that finally got her to see the truth."

Tristan leans forward and furrows his brow. "The truth about what?"

Brielle bites her bottom lip. She can't betray Cassandra's secret. "I can't say. It's not my truth to tell. It's hers."

Tristan's eyes bounce from side to side as he ponders, apparently putting the dots together. Then his brows lift. "You told me that you and Cassandra first fell out of touch because you accused Mr. Sinclair of something, and then he turned around and adopted her."

Brielle turns away, unwilling to confirm or deny his train of thought.

"Poor Cassandra," he sighs, breathing out all his hostility toward her in those two words.

"You can't mention anything to her," Brielle instantly declares. "I promised her I wouldn't say anything without her permission."

"And you didn't," he points out, arching a wry brow. "I won't say anything. But I can't promise I won't pay Mr. Sinclair a visit."

Her hand shoots up to tug on his arm. "Don't, Tristan. We have to let Cassandra handle this her own way. I tried to meddle and got flambéed."

He lets out a heavy sigh and nods. "Is there anything I can do for you? Ask for more painkillers? Or more pillows? Or get you something to drink?"

She shakes her head. "Just stay."

"I can do that." He settles more into his chair and leans over the bed, resting on his elbows and offering a comforting smile. "I have no intention of letting you out of my sight any time soon."

Heat shoots down her spine and swirls in her core like an oven, and Brielle feels perfectly content to stay in this hospital bed if it means having Tristan next to her.

Maybe, just for a little while, she can pretend.

CASSANDRA

"Come on, you can do better than that."

Tristan dodges Cassandra's punch and kicks her legs out from under her, making her land on her butt for the third time. She pushes down the pain that lances through her back, knowing it shouldn't hurt as much as it does. At least it's better than landing on her face.

Cassandra narrows her eyes and purses her lips in frustration as she looks up at him from the dirty ground inside the apartments. She's not used to losing, especially when she tries this hard. And he's not giving her any slack.

"I'm doing my best, but you're not giving me a chance," she protests, standing up and dusting herself off.

"Skins aren't in the business of giving chances either," he retorts with a wry brow. "Now, on your feet. Let's go again."

Rolling her eyes, she climbs back up. "Why do I even have to learn combat skills? What I should be doing is learning to control my powers. I could just blast the bad guys."

Tristan shakes his head. "You can't just go around throwing fire balls at people in broad daylight. Powers and suits are for last resorts, or when we know we're safe from exposure. You're right that you need to control your powers, especially after what you did to Brielle."

The words stab at her gut, and heat flushes her cheeks.

"Let's go one more round, then we'll work on both your powers and Jareth's. I have an exercise in mind. But first, come at me." He adopts a fighting stance and invites her to attack with a rigid wave of his outstretched hand.

Cassandra takes a step forward, clenching her jaw in determination to pummel him. With all the speed she uses on the track, she throws punch after kick after punch at him just the way he's shown her, but nothing lands. He's much faster.

She throws a punch and is met with his fist stopping right before her face.

"You need to keep your hand up to block your face," she hears him say as she shakes her head in an attempt to recover from the almost-blow.

Frustration burns in her chest, fueling the simmer in her palms. She's spent her whole life taking hits, and she's had enough.

She anchors her left fist against her cheek and retracts her right like she's about to punch. Tristan pivots left, so she lunges forward, using his sideways momentum against him to take him to the ground.

She lands on top of him, and his eyes are wide with surprise. Cassandra hovers over him, uncertain of what to do now that she's got him on the ground.

"Well done, Cassandra," he praises. "Not many people can say they took down Tristan Ayers."

Her lips curl in a haughty smile. "I knew I'd kick your butt eventually," she says, unable to keep the flirtatious lilt from her voice. From this angle, Tristan looks so yummy.

Suddenly, something reaches over her shoulder, and Tristan's shoe is in her face right before his leg pulls her backward, forcing her to topple off him. Pain explodes across her back. Pain that has nothing to do with Tristan's training.

Pain she needs to hide.

"Now you just need to work on your ground game," he says, and Cassandra can hear Jareth sighing over by the wall.

She rolls onto her knees and slaps her burning hands against the dirt, her blonde hair falling like a curtain over her face. "No fair, Tristan," she snaps.

He stands and dusts himself off. "Skins don't play fair," he responds with a shrug that's trying to hide the smirk curling the edges of his lips. He offers his hand, and she ruefully accepts it and lets him help her up.

"Alright, Jareth, you're in, too," he calls.

Jareth kicks himself away from the wall he was leaning against and joins them.

"Now Jareth, your goal is to create objects as fast as you can and hurl them at Cassandra," Tristan instructs. "And Cassandra, your job is to blast them before they hit you."

Cassandra's pulse quickens in anticipation, and her heels start to bounce of their own accord. Finally, something fun!

"What should I throw at her?" Jareth asks, a questioning shrug lifting his shoulders.

"Something heavy, like a piano," Tristan replies, "or an elephant."

"Maybe an anchor," Jareth adds.

"Hey!" Cassandra complains.

Both guys chuckle.

"How about pillows," Tristan suggests in earnest. "Or anything that won't totally cripple her if she misses."

"Ok, so just a mild maiming," Jareth says. "Gotcha."

"Watch it, Capricorn, or I'll scorch you next," Cassandra warns, pointing her index finger at him like she's aiming a pistol.

She walks to the opposite side of the room and turns to

face him. "Let's do this," she invites with a flare of her left brow.

Accepting her challenge, Jareth raises a hand, and in the blink of an eye, a red rubber ball manifests. Is that a dodgeball? He hurls it at Cassandra, and she instinctively throws her hand toward it, releasing a bright blast of sunlight that annihilates the ball into a burst of cinders.

One after the other, he throws dozens of balls at her in different ways, and she blasts each of them, feeling like Spiderman shooting his web, only this is way more satisfying. It feels oddly exhilarating to destroy things. It makes her feel powerful. Like there's nothing she can't do. Like she doesn't ever have to fear anything or anyone again.

They pause, both of them panting with exertion.

"Woo! That was the coolest game of dodgeball I've ever seen!" Tristan hoots and applauds.

A buzzing sounds in the twilight, and Tristan fumbles in his pocket to remove his phone. "You guys take a break," he says before answering it and walking off into a corner.

"Must be Brielle," Jareth says, nodding his head toward Tristan as he closes the distance between them. "Whenever he hears from her, his eyes light up."

She crosses her arms and looks at Tristan. "What's the deal with him and Brielle anyway? They're clearly both crazy about each other. Why aren't they together?"

Jareth shakes his head and sighs. "I know what you mean. I can see how the separation stings both of them, and being the third person in a room with them is weird." He chuckles, then immediately sobers, looking at Tristan. "It's because the other Gemini Guardian is out there somewhere."

"Huh?" Cassandra turns confused eyes on Jareth. "Other Gemini Guardian?"

He nods. "Gemini for some reason has two guardians, each half of a whole. Tristan tells me the other one is supposed to be his soulmate. That's why he keeps Brielle at arm's length. He doesn't want to get close to her only to have to break her heart later."

"Oh," she says slowly, and every tense and strained moment she's witnessed between Tristan and Brielle replays in her head. Followed by her every attempt to flirt with Tristan and steal his attention. Shame flushes red heat up her neck. "Poor Brielle," she says, more to herself.

"I know," Jareth says, then stiffens and looks away.

Cassandra hears the crunch of Tristan's feet coming closer.

"That was Brielle," he says like they hadn't already guessed. "She's coming home this evening. Let's go ahead and cut this session short. As soon as she calls, I'm heading to her place."

Cassandra's shoulders drop in disappointment. Things were just getting good!

"Hey, why don't we go grab a bite while you wait," Jareth suggests. "Better than you sitting at home by yourself having a staring contest with your phone."

Tristan frowns and Jareth smirks. "I guess."

"Good, because Veronica is waiting for us at the diner," Jareth adds.

Tristan chuckles and rolls his eyes, shoving his hands in his pockets. "Come on, Cassandra," he says, nodding his head toward the door. "I'll buy you a treat for knocking you on your butt so much."

She narrows her eyes at him, then flips her hair over her shoulder. "Sure, why not?"

The table is quiet as the four of them sit there. Tristan spinning his phone on the table, waiting for it to ring. Jareth and Veronica making goo-goo eyes at each other and pretending no one else exists. And Cassandra refusing to eat what this place calls pie, trying not to think about her dad.

After staying with Brielle at the hospital until midnight Thursday, Cassandra had completely forgotten that he was most likely waiting for her so they could "discuss" her performance at the track meet. By the time she got home, his anger had turned from red to pitch black, and she wished she hadn't gone home at all.

He whipped her back ten times with his belt, and promised that it would happen again every single night until she "did better". She'd prayed it was an empty threat.

It wasn't.

Every day she came home, and every night he beat her. Her back was so swollen, she couldn't even sit back against the leather booth. That was only part of the reason she'd sucked so bad at the training sessions with Tristan. The slightest contact to her back was excruciating, and Tristan held nothing back. But she can't tell him. So, she's just had to endure it.

If there's one thing Cassandra can do better than anyone, it's endure.

The silence in the lazy diner is broken by gasps and chatter from the staff behind the counter. Cassandra looks up from her sad cherry pie to see a heavy-set waitress frantically aiming a remote at the TV attached to the corner of the wall two booths down from theirs.

The volume dial on the screen climbs until Cassandra can hear the voice of the news anchor.

"Reports have just come in that NASA has detected an asteroid heading our way," the well-dressed brunette says in a robotic tone.

Cassandra leans forward in her seat, causing the others at the table to turn and look at the TV.

"The asteroid is estimated to be the size of Texas," the anchor continues, and a video box appears beside her head depicting a rock the size of the lone star state. In the next few seconds, the video changes to shrink the rock to a dot in space next to Earth. "According to NASA's calculations, the asteroid is on a collision course with the Moon."

This time, the whole diner gasps in chorus.

Cassandra shakes her head. This has to be some kind of joke. This can't actually be happening.

"When?" Tristan curses under his breath, slamming his clenched fist on the table.

"Scientists can't say for sure, but the estimated time to impact is five days," reports the anchor, as if replying directly to Tristan. "But NASA assures the country that they are working with space corporations around the world to rectify the situation. Officials urge everyone above all not to panic. Continue about your lives as you normally would, and treasure your time with your loved ones. As soon as there is any further news on the topic, we will report it immediately."

Cassandra feels suddenly cold, like all the blood has drained from her face and extremities. The clinking of china against the table top as Tristan slams his fist down diverts her attention.

"Chardis," he growls.

"Are you sure?" asks a frightened Veronica.

"If Chardis could do that, why wouldn't he have done it seventeen years ago?" Jareth asks, squeezing Veronica closer to him.

"He didn't know where we were seventeen years ago," Tristan responds. "My guess is, once he figured it out, he's been waiting for us to come of age and discover our powers, so that he can flush us out of hiding with a move like this. Force us to take action so that we expose ourselves."

Suddenly, all of Cassandra's worldly worries seem petty. Her irritation with training, her fear over going home. Her popularity, what college she chooses, none of that matters now.

All that matters is saving the planet, not just for her sake, but for the sake of everyone.

She locks Tristan's gaze with determination. "What do we do?"

JACK

11:40

Jack picks up his bottle of antacids only to find it's empty. Of course it is. He slams it back down on his desk, grabbing his cup of cold coffee instead.

McNally's disappeared again.

Of course he has. Add that to the news that a mysterious asteroid is heading for the moon, and he has the cherry on the crap-cake that today is. All he can do is wait. Wait for McNally to reappear. Wait to see what NASA plans to do about the asteroid.

And Jack hates waiting.

Clara types away at the desk beside him and Jack wonders what she's doing. They don't have any leads. Any sightings. Any clues as to where to search next.

And according to some, life on Earth is about to end.

His cell rings and Jack's brows hike up when he sees it's a silent number. "Yes?" he answers curtly.

"We need to meet."

Jack glances over at Clara, but she seems focused. Turning his back, he lowers his voice. "What have you got?"

"Not over the phone," his informant hisses. "You free?"

"I can make time," Jack answers, trying not to let himself get hopeful. This guy's never asked to meet.

"Good. I'm in the café downstairs. Table at the back."

The line goes dead and Jack frowns. He's here? Now?

Curiosity piqued, he grabs his jacket.

"Everything okay?" Clara asks as she watches him put it on.

"Yep." Jack holds up his coffee cup. "Going to get one that doesn't taste like mud. I know you don't drink the fuel that powers most of this globe, but is there anything else you'd like?"

"I'm fine." Clara's face softens. "Thanks for remembering."

"Sure."

Jack turns away, conscious that his cheeks have heated against his will. He strides to the elevator, telling himself to get a grip. Clara is after a promotion, nothing else.

Down on the ground floor, the café is just starting to fill up with the lunch crowd. Jack strides past the counter. He refuses to pay for something as essential as air. The tables at the back are largely empty. An elderly couple are sharing a pot of tea. A young mother is sipping her toddler's babyccino.

At the far table sits a pudgy young man with thick glasses. Not exactly what Jack imagined a street-hardened informant to look like, but the guy lifts a hand in acknowledgement.

Taking a seat, Jack notes the wispy hairs on the man's chin. "You know this is unusual."

Informants prefer to keep their identity a secret, and agents prefer it that way. The less they're associated with them, the better.

The guy shrugs. "Do I look normal to you?"

Jack raises a brow and waits, mentally cataloguing the guy's rumpled shirt and unbrushed hair.

"The name's Alexei, by the way. Thanks for meeting me."

"Sure," Jack says, still waiting.

Alexei raises a brow. "So, the Mr. Taciturn wasn't just a phone thing, huh?"

Jack goes to get up. He wishes he could say he doesn't have time for this, but there's no point lying if he doesn't need to. "Look—"

"Alexei."

Jack sighs. "Alexei. I'm not sure why we had to do this face to face, but—"

"Because phone calls can be traced, Jack. And what I need to tell you has to stay off the record."

Jack drops back into his chair. "Everything we discuss is off the record."

Alexei shakes his head as if Jack's being naïve. "You never know who's watching, when."

Tensing, Jack's eyes flick around the café, unsure whether he wants more eyes or less in here right now. More eyes mean witnesses if Alexei isn't planning on playing nice. Less eyes mean fewer people know this meeting ever happened.

"I've already checked," Alexei assures him. "The place isn't bugged. The feds are too arrogant to think these sorts of conversations can happen within their own headquarters."

"What sort of conversations?"

Alexei leans forward. "The organization I work for, we've discovered some…anomalies."

That has Jack's attention. Anomalies? And what organization? The same one Tristan claims his parents were part of? "I'm listening," he states flatly.

"Our scanners detected changes in dark matter near Earth some time ago. We've been monitoring it closely."

Jack waits again, giving himself time to process this. It appears Alexei's with NASA.

"The changes occurred right where the asteroid appeared.

We're doing everything we can to make sure that hunk of rock doesn't make it to the moon."

"This all sounds intriguing, Alexei, and just like every other person on this planet, I'm hoping you're successful. But I'm not sure why you're telling me. The FBI can't help you with this."

"No, but you may be able to help us."

"I have no desire to work for NASA, but I appreciate the interest."

Alexei shakes his head. "I don't exactly work for NASA."

For some reason, the way Alexei's voice dips has Jack's gut clenching. He narrows his eyes. "Who do you work for?"

Alexei's eyes dart right and left, his wispy beard twitching. "I belong to a secret organization. We employ professionals from a wide variety of disciplines, including NASA and FBI." He looks Jack in the eye, his voice low. "Nebula is an agency that monitors extra-terrestrial activity and protects earth from alien attacks."

Jack exhales and promptly forgets to inhale. There are others out there who understand the threats Earth could face. There's an organization determined to uncover the same truths he is.

Nebula.

Alexei's gaze hasn't wavered. "We've been watching you for a while now, Jack. We believe our interests may overlap with yours. We'd like you to join us."

Jack doesn't even blink. "I'm in."

25

TRISTAN

The TV screens in HQ have been permanently on since the breaking news.

An asteroid is heading for the moon. One that Tristan has no doubt Chardis launched through the wormhole.

If there aren't images of the giant rock hurtling through space, then it's of the panic that's spreading like a disease around the world. Store shelves are empty as people prepare for living in a post-apocalyptic world. Schools are deserted as people keep their children home and everyone realizes what was really important all along. Suicide rates have spiked amongst those who are less hopeful about how this could turn out.

Tristan's about to press the mute button when the news anchor announces something new for a change. "We have Dr. Antonov from the National Aeronautics and Space Administration joining us in just a moment for an exclusive interview. Hopefully we'll be able to get some answers detailing NASA's response to this unprecedented turn of events."

The Zodiacs crowd around Tristan and he shifts a little closer to Brielle. He's so glad her parents let her come over after leaving the hospital. Having her here makes this somehow easier, slightly less horrifying. Who knows whether this exclusive is going to be good news or not.

A new face appears on the screen and everyone glances at each other. The guy's pudgy and young, with some half-beard sprouting on his chin. Far too young to be called a doctor.

The news anchor blinks. "Good morning, ah, Dr. Antonov."

"Please, call me Alexei," says the guy with a smile. "Doctor just makes me feel old. Unlike my more senior colleagues, I earned my PhD in astrophysics at the age of twenty-four."

The woman blinks again. "Of course. So, what can you tell us about this asteroid, Dr…, Alexei?"

"Well, as many of you have been learning, asteroids are space debris. Larger asteroids, as this one is, can also be called planetoids or minor planets."

"So a minor planet is on a collision course with our moon?"

Alexei beams at her. "That's exactly what's happening, Sofia."

"How did NASA not know of this? Shouldn't we have been warned sooner?"

"Space is a mysterious place, Sofia. It's always throwing curve balls at us, this time, quite literally."

Sofia looks like she's trying not to frown. She glances down at the sheets of paper before her. "And if this…minor planet were to hit our moon, what would that mean for Earth?"

Alexei's whiskers are practically twitching. "Well, that would depend on whether the impact of the collision moves the moon closer to Earth or further away. What do you understand of the moon's current impact on Earth, Sofia?"

"Well." Sofia swallows. The poor woman probably wasn't

expecting a high school science quiz when she slipped behind her news desk. "The moon affects our tides."

"Not just a pretty face, huh?" Alexei praises. "As you just said, the moon has its own gravity, which pulls the oceans toward it."

Sofia straightens a little, even though she didn't actually mention gravity.

"If that gravitational pull comes closer, it's going to become stronger, potentially up to four hundred times greater than what we have now. A mighty tidal bulge would be created, causing great flooding, with cities such as London and New York disappearing under water. Of course, when the moon moves on, the flooding will subside as the water retreats," Alexei assures, as if that will make everything okay.

"And if the moon moves further away?" Sofia squeaks.

"That will be equally as disastrous. The moon keeps the Earth at its current rate of rotation. If the Earth were to slow down too much then this would lead to a more extreme tilt to the polar axis, and with it would come increasingly extreme weather. We'd be looking at some pretty hot summers, sub-arctic winters, and widespread ecosystem extinctions."

Veronica moves closer to Jareth as Cassandra crosses her arms. Beside Tristan, Brielle is still and silent. He wishes he could take her hand. They'd weave their fingers together, a physical reminder they're not facing this alone.

That there's a chance they can stop this.

"You seem to be quite calm about this, Alexei." Although the news anchor's face maintains her curious impassivity, there's a hint of censure in her voice.

Understatement, Sofia. Alexei almost looks like he's considering putting bets down as to which outcome it is.

"Well, that's because NASA doesn't intend for either of these outcomes to eventuate."

Sofia leans forward, probably like everyone at home is right now. "Yes?"

"NASA is planning on launching a missile. That asteroid is going to be little more than space dust sprinkling the surface of the moon."

Before Tristan can take stock of what the others think of this, his vision contracts. Impenetrable black appears at the edges, quickly consuming the room around him.

Drawing a sharp breath, he stills, knowing he can't fight what's coming.

"Tristan?" Brielle asks, her voice filled with concern.

But Tristan can't answer. Reality is being swallowed by something else.

A vision of the future.

For the first time in his life, he finds himself in space. Infinite, endless, star-studded space. It stretches in every direction, horizonless everywhere he looks. Pricks of light dot the inky black, feeling like they repeat over and over, exponentially. Infinitely.

Never has Tristan felt so small.

His eyes widen. Or breakable as he sees what's coming toward him.

A mammoth, spinning space rock. It's hurtling at a speed he's never seen before, multiplying in size with every blink. Instinctively, Tristan goes to move, realizing he's directly in its path.

But he can't.

Only his mind is here, not his body.

Reflexively, he throws his arms in front of his face a moment before impact. A breathless second later, he doesn't feel a thing. Opening his eyes, Tristan realizes the asteroid went straight through him as if he wasn't here.

Because he's not.

He spins around to watch it continue its path, and his eyes widen again.

"No," he whispers.

The impact of the asteroid colliding with the moon is explosive. It crashes through Tristan like a physical force, vibrating down his nerves. The asteroid shatters, shards of rock flinging into the blackness.

A massive crater appears on the moon as it jolts. Tristan reaches out as if he can grab it, as if he can try to stop what's about to happen, but the gray ball of rock jerks like it was just shoved. The moon spins on its axis as it propels through space, waiting for the momentum to stop in this place where gravity doesn't exist.

Tristan's arm drops. Thanks to Alexei, he now knows what this will mean for Earth. A dialed-up greenhouse effect —extreme weather, mass extinctions across the globe. Millions will die.

The scene dissolves and Tristan turns back. There's no time to catch his breath, to try and process what he just witnessed, because the asteroid is coming at him again.

The second vision has begun.

He doesn't lift his arms up this time, just watches and waits as the mammoth rock propels through space. Who knows how this one will end. What he's about to see.

Still, as the asteroid makes like a freight train straight for him, Tristan finds himself tensing. Something the size of a state is about to railroad through where he's standing, whether he has a physical body or not.

But the asteroid never reaches him. A blast of light has Tristan looking left. A missile is rocketing like a shooting star, its trajectory aimed straight for the asteroid. It spears toward it like a burning, deadly arrow. The tip connects with the asteroid and Tristan holds his breath.

This explosion will be full of fire and blinding light. The asteroid will never stand a chance.

"Should we do something?" Cassandra's worried voice infiltrates his consciousness.

"I don't think so," Jareth murmurs. "He has to see this through."

What? No! If Tristan can hear voices, then the vision is about it to end.

It dissolves before the thought is finished. Before Tristan gets to see the explosion of the decade. Maybe century.

Probably millennia.

HQ seems dim and small compared to where Tristan just was. Almost unfamiliar.

Breathing heavily, he works to orient himself. To try and understand what he saw. The first vision…

A hand touches his arm and his heart rate instantly slows. Looking down, he finds Brielle beside him, quiet and concerned. Tristan uses her moss-green gaze to anchor himself. To remind himself that they can't have come this far, only for them to lose.

"What did you see?" she asks, warmth and worry filling her gaze.

Realizing he's leaning toward her, Tristan quickly pulls back and turns to look at the others. "In one scenario, NASA launches their missile. The vision ended, but it looks like it obliterates the asteroid."

Cassandra lets out a breath. "That's good news."

But Brielle is still watching Tristan. "And the other scenario?"

"There is no missile." Tristan swallows. "The asteroid hits the moon and propels it further away from Earth."

The others stand in silence, blinking. Cassandra is the first to recover. "And there's no way to know—"

"No," Tristan states flatly. "There's no way to tell which

vision is the true future. Believe me, my parents and I tried to figure out whether there was some kind of pattern, some kind of way to differentiate them."

And they always came up with nothing.

Cassandra nods, then crosses her arms.

Simultaneously, the Zodiacs turn to face the TV, knowing this is all they can do right now.

Watch.

And wait.

BRIELLE

Though the fluorescent lights are bright in the windowless room, Brielle can feel that the world outside is dark. She's been here for hours, sitting as close to Tristan as he'll let her while they watch the news, soaking up the comfort of his proximity. Every news broadcast they see is either lively speculation about the asteroid or coverage of the resultant mayhem in larger cities—widespread theft of electronics and pharmaceutical drugs, grocery stores selling out of water, paper products and canned goods, senseless acts of violence.

Brielle had been so looking forward to getting out of the hospital. Laying in that bed for days, idly channel surfing in between visits from the nurses to check her burns and redress the bandages, which was an excruciating task each time; she's not looking forward to having to change them herself from now on.

Little did she know that the threat of impending doom was waiting for her when she finally got released. Frank and Bea reluctantly let her go to Tristan's only because she begged, and though they haven't hastened her with any texts or calls, she knows they're likely eagerly waiting for her to come home.

"I'd better get going," Cassandra says, finally breaking the long silence. "I'm honestly surprised my parents haven't called yet, but I'm sure they're freaking out about all this."

"Yeah, I should get home, too," Veronica adds. "Make sure Logan doesn't turn into a crazy hoarder before Dad gets home."

Jareth stands as the girls do. "I'll take you both home," he volunteers. "It's too dangerous out there for you to be taking the bus."

Cassandra rolls her eyes and offers a slightly patronizing smile. "Thanks for the chivalry, but I have my own car, remember?"

"Ah, right," Jareth says with a shrug, then turns to Brielle. "Need a ride?"

Brielle stands, too, her body stiff from sitting in the same chair all afternoon. "Sure. I think I've kept Frank and Bea waiting long enough."

Jareth smiles. "Cool—"

"Actually, I'll take her home," Tristan interrupts, springing to his feet.

They all turn surprised and curious eyes on him, especially Brielle.

He slides his hands into his pockets, pushing up his shoulders, feigning nonchalance.

After an awkward second without an excuse from Tristan, Jareth finally says, "Okay. Well…see you guys later." He drapes an arm over Veronica's shoulders and they both frown questioningly at Tristan as they walk out the door.

Cassandra, on the other hand, smirks wryly, cat eyes bouncing between Tristan and Brielle. "Later," she calls, then winks at Brielle before making her typical supermodel exit.

Brielle and Tristan are now alone in HQ, and she can't

keep her heart from doing somersaults wondering what's going through his mind.

"So, there's something I've been meaning to give you," Tristan says, a strange note of excitement in his voice. "I didn't do it earlier because everyone was here, and I thought it merited privacy."

He rushes to a photograph of his parents and swings one side away from the wall, revealing a hidden safe. He enters in the code and opens the door, withdraws something, then closes it again, returning the frame to its original position on the wall.

Sitting in front of her, he opens his hand to reveal a familiar vial containing an unforgettable yellow liquid.

Brielle's breath catches in her throat as she stares at it. Then she lifts questioning eyes up to meet his. "You're giving me nanites?" Her voice is so breathless it's barely more than a whisper.

He nods, placing the vial in her hands.

"No, I can't take that," she insists, trying to push it back into his grasp. "This is for life or death situations. I'm not dying, I don't need them. It would be a waste—"

Tristan shakes his head, closing both his hands around hers and the vial as he pushes them back towards her. "I'm not going to let you suffer for weeks as your burns heal into massive scars. You deserve better than that. Not to mention we need you well for whatever comes next. And I still have plenty of vials. I won't miss one."

He drops his hands, and she looks down at the liquid that swirls inside the glass like it's alive.

"I wanted to give it to you right away," he says. "I brought one to the hospital with me when I first got the call, just in case you were in critical condition. But once I saw that you were...in one piece, I knew it was too risky. The nurses would have freaked if you healed that quickly. It would have raised too much suspicion. So I promised myself I'd make you drink it as soon as you got out, no matter how much you argued."

He grins teasingly and winks, but still all she can do is stare at him with wide eyes.

It feels so selfish to take this, when one of them—especially Tristan—might need it in the future. She'll heal from these burns. It'll take a few months, but she'll be fine. She's not thrilled about the idea of having scars the rest of her life, but she's not so vain that she'd sacrifice saving a future life.

"I know that look," he says, frowning. "If you refuse, I'll get it in you somehow. Don't make me slip into one of your drinks when you're not looking." His expression is playful but his eyes are serious.

A nervous laugh trips out of her shaky lungs.

"Take it," he softly implores. "Please."

With that word, all her resistance dissolves. When has she ever been able to deny Tristan anything?

She unscrews the cap with trembling fingers and slowly lifts the vial up to her lips.

Without worrying it will taste bad, she throws back her head and lets the yellow liquid slide down her throat. The texture is strangely slimy and leaves a bitter aftertaste on the back of her tongue, making her want to gag. She swallows repeatedly to soothe the urge, refusing to waste such a precious gift out of reflex.

The gelatinous goo crawls down her esophagus, warming her chest as it descends, and she feels gross, like she's just ingested a handful of living worms. Screwing on the cap, she pushes the thought away, desperate not to repulse herself.

Tristan gives her hand a squeeze before he takes the empty vial.

"Thank you," she says, hoping he understands just how much she appreciates this gesture.

"I should be thanking you," he says. "Here I thought I'd have to pin you down and make you drink it." He laughs, and the idea of Tristan tackling her and pinning her under him makes her wish she'd given more of a fight. She blushes and turns away.

"Let's get you home before Frank calls the cops on me," he says.

She follows Tristan to the garage, and he opens the passenger door of his truck for her. Her chest stings as she pulls herself up into the seat, but there's a new sensation, too. A subtle tingle all throughout the skin, like there's a static current spanning from one upper arm to the other.

The nanites are already working!

Brielle isn't sure why that surprises her. She'd watched Tristan quickly bounce back from the fight against Adalind and her Skins after he'd drank the nanites. And he'd been in worse condition than her, that's for sure.

Tristan gets in beside her and starts the truck, then pulls out onto the road.

"Are you okay?" he asks, glancing at her.

She hadn't been aware just how deeply she's frowning, or how wide her eyes are, until hearing Tristan's concern. She relaxes her features.

"I'm fine, more than fine," she reassures excitedly. "It just…tingles. I didn't think it would work so quickly."

A warm smile spreads across his gorgeous lips. "Yeah, it does feel weird. There are really no words I could use to describe the sensation that would do it justice."

She nods, paying attention to each spot where the tingle intensifies and comparing it with her mental map of the burns. It definitely seems like the feeling is stronger in the places the burns were the worst.

All of a sudden, the tingling subsides, and she feels nothing under the bandages. Fueled by a new need for verification, Brielle looks down at her chest, tugging at the top of her shirt and the gauze. But neither will give enough leverage for even a peek.

She has to see it with her own eyes, has to know for sure that the burns are really gone. And she has to know right now.

"Tristan, I think it's healed!" she exclaims. "I need to see it, before I go home, so Frank and Bea won't see. Will you stop the truck and help me unwrap the bandages?"

Tristan doesn't argue. He slowly pulls over onto the grassy side of the country road, all the while stealing sideways glances at her that are full of curiosity, and something else.

As soon as the truck's in park, Brielle pulls her t-shirt over her head, bouncing in her seat with anticipation.

Tristan reaches out to her with slow, uncertain hands, and in her urgency, she leans forward to give him better access. His warm fingers find the end of the gauze and begin to unwrap it, passing it to her so she can wind it around the side he can't reach, and then back again. Her eyes are glued downward, watching anxiously as more and more skin is exposed.

Smooth, unblemished skin!

Pale pink, un-blackened skin!

At last, the gauze is fully unwrapped, her neck, shoulders and top of her bosom exposed above the line of her simple strapless bra.

"Wow," she and Tristan chorus.

Her chest looks just the way it always did, without a single scar or scab. It was like the incident with Cassandra never happened.

She'd been trying to tell herself it was okay that she'd have scars forever, that she was never a great beauty anyway, that real beauty was only skin deep. All those cliches about looks that people say when the truth isn't pretty.

But she knew. Those scars would have always haunted her, made her feel ugly. She already did her best to stay under most people's radar, but the scars would have made her feel like she had to be invisible to avoid offending anyone, to avoid injuring her fragile self-esteem with their reactions.

Now, those once inevitabilities will never be an issue.

Relief as powerful and forceful as a tsunami crashes over her, and she's helpless against the tears that spill down her cheeks and onto the impossibly healed skin she can't stop staring at.

"I can't believe it's all gone," she weeps, the happy sobs coming out like laughs.

"Don't cry." Tristan's knuckles suddenly graze the side of her cheek, and his thumb wipes at the fresh tears.

Ready to profess her immense gratitude, she looks up at him, but the intense, heated twinkle simmering in his blue eyes erases everything else from her mind.

For the first time, she's aware that she's alone with Tristan in his truck in only her bra. There's a voice whispering in the back of her mind that she needs to cover herself, but she can barely hear it. All she can do is stare into those eyes that are holding her prisoner.

His hand slowly moves downward, the back of his fingers trailing down her face, her chin. Her neck. His fingertips lightly brush the center of her collarbone, and her eyes close as she shudders from the electric sizzle his touch sends throughout her body.

"So beautiful..." he whispers.

The space between them decreases, his face coming closer and closer, as if their two bodies are being pulled closer by a magnetic force, one that neither of them has the will to fight.

His lips are her new focal point, entrancing her gaze, pulling her closer with their promised sweetness, and she knows it's only a matter of nanoseconds before they're touching hers. The knowledge kicks her heart rate into hyperdrive.

Their noses touch, and her dazed eyelids fall, her breath pausing in eager anticipation.

Buzz, buzz!

The quiet vibration is piercing in the heavy silence, and they both jump as if shocked awake by a defibrillator. When they recover, they each settle back into their seats, the distance seeming great and cold.

Clumsy fingers find her phone in her front pocket, and Brielle answers it without remembering to check who it is first.

"H-hello?" she stammers, disoriented.

"Hey, I don't want to rush you home, but, uh…" It's Frank.

"Oh, yeah, I'm actually on my way now," she replies. "I'll be there soon."

"Ok, great, see you shortly," Frank says before hanging up.

Brielle's cheeks are burning like embers as she puts her phone back into her pocket and reaches for her shirt on the dash.

She and Tristan almost just kissed! Frank's timing couldn't have been worse—or better, if you ask Frank.

"I guess I'd better start driving again." Tristan rubs the back of his neck, his voice raspy.

"Oh, uh, could you help first?" She holds up the wadded gauze. "There are multiple reasons why Frank and Bea will freak out if they see me not wearing this."

Even in the dark, Brielle can see Tristan's cheeks redden.

"Oh, right. Sure." He takes the gauze and she helps him wrap it around her no longer marred chest.

She can't help but notice that his gaze bounces everywhere but on her chest, which only makes her blush even deeper. How did this moment become so painfully awkward?

As soon as he's done, she pulls her shirt back on and buckles back in. She keeps her face fixed toward the windshield in front of her, too mortified to look at him. Somehow, she can tell he's avoiding looking at her, too.

It seems like only seconds later when they pull into her driveway.

"Thanks again, Tristan," she says as she opens the door, stealing a glance at him before she hops down to the pavement.

"Yep, see you tomorrow," he says quickly with a curt wave, meeting her eyes for the briefest moment before they both look away.

She skips up the front door, hearing Tristan's truck back out and swiftly drive away.

Once inside, she leans against the closed door and sighs heavily.

If only Frank hadn't called.

27

TRISTAN

Pitch.
          Pitch.
    Pitch.

Tristan wipes his hand down his face for the hundredth time since he left Brielle's. What in the world was he thinking?

He wasn't. That's the problem. He was just…feeling.

Lost to emotions and sensations that were impossible to resist. Like a tide. Or gravity.

Or the need to draw in the next breath.

Turning a corner, he's about to swipe down his face again —as if he can wipe away the scent of her, the wish that the cell phone had never rung—when he slams on the brakes.

The main drag of Mirror Point is so congested that he nearly rammed up the rear end of a boat. Tristan frowns, realizing that's exactly what's in front of him.

A boat that's behind another truck, perched on a trailer. Tristan peers closer. The boat is stacked high with crates and boxes…and toilet paper. Looks like Noah is ready for the flood.

Stretching so he can see past it, Tristan takes in the long row of taillights. People are running in and out of shops, trailers and truck beds are stacked high with anything and everything. Some people have staples. Others seem to have packed up their entire household and are leaving.

Mirror Point is in a panic, no doubt like the rest of the world.

Tristan flicks on the radio. He stopped listening after NASA made their announcement—every channel was now just repeating what everyone knows.

An asteroid is heading to the moon.

If it hits, life as they know it will end.

Tristan clamps his hands around the steering wheel. What they aren't able to broadcast, because no one else knows, is that a determined evil is the one who set this into motion.

And even if the asteroid is destroyed, it will only be the beginning.

The radio crackles to life, but no music greets Tristan; instead it's a somber voice outlining the chaos that is steadily descending across the globe. Bottled water stocks have disappeared from supermarket shelves. Canned goods are scarce. Entire aisles are bare.

People are moving in masses, many to higher ground because they're terrified of super-tides, others have decided they simply want to be closer to family. The ones who can't afford to leave, or have no way of getting out, are preparing for violence.

Tristan idles where he is for several minutes. When he realizes he won't be moving anytime soon, he pulls over to the curb. There's no way he's sitting in a stationary vehicle for who-knows-how-long listening to this stuff, with nothing but frustration to accompany him.

No, it's not just frustration. Alongside the twitchy, hot

feeling is something quiet and still. Regret. Regret he's not even sure he understands.

Is he disappointed that he almost kissed Brielle?

Or does he wish that they were never interrupted?

Not wanting to know the answer, Tristan starts walking. He has no idea where he's going, all he knows is he needs to move.

His legs take long strides, the type where he wishes he could break into a jog. Maybe a sprint. It's like he's running from a Skin.

Worse. He's running from himself.

Ducking and weaving around the panicked faces rushing around him, Tristan sees he's beside Creamy Dreams. Deciding that a sugar hit is just what he needs, he slips inside.

Only to come up short.

Madge is standing behind the counter, her hands up in the air. A short man wearing what looks like three backpacks strapped to his back and front is on the other side, wielding a baseball bat.

"Hurry up," he growls. "Get it for me. Now."

Although Madge's whole body is trembling, she doesn't move. She's rooted to the spot in fear.

"Hurry up!" the man screams. "Others will be coming."

Tristan steps forward. "Too late. Someone else is already here."

The man startles and leaps back so he has both Madge and Tristan in view. "Stay back! I don't want any trouble."

Tristan raises a brow. "And you didn't think of that before you threatened a lady with a bat?"

The man swings it wildly and Madge jumps back. "Stay away or I'll be forced to use it!"

Tristan stays where he is. "Look, everything could be okay, yet. There's no need to do this just for a few dollars."

"Money," the man screeches. "You think I'm doing this for money?"

Tristan makes a show of looking quizzical, surreptitiously taking a step forward. He waves toward the empty fridge that usually houses the drinks. "Well, all the bottled water is gone."

The bat drops a few inches as the man shakes his head. "I'm here for Oreos!"

Tristan blinks, not sure he heard that right. This man is staking a hold up for cream cookies?

"Food will be the world's new currency," the man shouts, panic trying to override his conviction. "High calorie foods. Ones that can last years."

Yep, sounds like Oreos.

"Stealing, on the other hand, won't be," Tristan points out, slipping a few inches forward. Madge is slowly shifting away from the counter, gaze darting between Tristan and her attacker.

The guy slides a glance at Tristan. "I'll give you a quarter of what I get."

Tristan snorts. "First of all, that's a terrible deal. Second, they're not even the choc caramel flavor."

The man frowns, lifting the bat again, but Tristan continues.

"And third, it's time to put the bat down."

The man's mouth snaps open, clearly intending on refusing, although he never gets a chance.

Tristan picks up the metal napkin holder on the table he's standing beside and throws it. It spears through the air like a bullet, slamming into the top of the baseball bat. It hits with such force that the wood cracks and splinters.

The man jumps back, dropping the bat in shock. Seeing the opening he was hoping for, Tristan leaps, grabbing him by two of the multiple backpack straps over the man's shoulders.

The man instantly cowers. "I wasn't going to hurt her! I promise!"

Tristan jerks him away from the counter, and the man stumbles limply. Shoving him toward the door, Tristan releases him. The man's propelled forward and he crashes into the door.

"Get out of here," Tristan growls. "And go buy your Oreos like everyone else."

With a brief, frightened look over his shoulder, the man opens the door and runs out.

Tristan picks up the bat, inspecting the broken end. The napkin holder left a dent, a crack zigzagging down the side, and some missing shards.

He presses his lips together. "I was kind of hoping it would smash it in the same way the missile will the asteroid—like it was symbolic, or something. I was trying to make a point."

Madge rushes out from behind the counter. "That was amazing! The fact that you're my hero is the point."

Tristan blinks. He hadn't considered this outcome when he rushed in.

Madge moves closer, her bleached ponytail skewed. "Thank you, Tristan."

He clears his throat, not entirely comfortable with the way Madge's eyes have rounded and softened. "People are going crazy with this asteroid. We just need to have more faith that it's all going to work out."

"But...what if it won't?" Madge asks quietly

Then Tristan should've kissed Brielle.

He shakes his head, mostly because of the unbidden, and unwanted, thought. "This isn't how it ends."

Chardis can't win this round.

He just can't.

Madge sighs. "If only I was a few years younger…" She reaches forward and Tristan tenses, but she simply pats him on the shoulder. "You should go home to that girl of yours. Now's the time to be with those you care the most about."

Tristan freezes. Brielle's face floats through his mind, making his heart stutter. She was so close. So beautiful. So impossible to deny.

Except that kiss being stopped is exactly what should've happened. Because, despite their undeniable chemistry, they're not soulmates.

And Tristan can't ever forget that. Losing sight of the fact his other half is out there somewhere, a vital key in defeating Chardis, is just too dangerous.

It could mean the difference between life and death for entire galaxies.

A wry smile twists across his lips. "Maybe lock up for the night, Madge," he suggests.

Madge nods. "I was just doing that. Impending doom isn't great for business."

Taking the bat with him, Tristan leaves. He's just stepping outside when he has to yank back. Someone precariously balancing a stack of bottled water rushes past, oblivious that he almost cleaned Tristan up.

Shaking his head, Tristan makes his way back to his truck. He'll take the backroads home.

And as he sits there, alone, watching the news for updates, he'll have to pretend an idea just didn't creep into his mind and start tapping an impatient foot.

If this is the end, if this is all finished before the Zodiacs even had a chance to begin, then what difference does it make?

Why can't he just give in and kiss Brielle?

JACK

21:17

Jack paces outside the FBI building, wondering what the hell he's thinking. He should've asked Alexei more questions before he agreed to meet him.

And join Nebula.

No investigator worth his salt would sign up for something he has no idea about. One mention of aliens though, and Jack was ready to sign. With blood, if needed. Just because all these years, he's done this alone. He's been labelled crazy because he wasn't willing to back down from what he knew was true.

But still. It doesn't mean he agrees and asks questions later. He has Logan and Veronica to consider. What if he just put himself in danger?

The sound of whistling has Jack spinning around to find Alexei ambling toward him, hands in his pockets. He waves jovially, as if he and Jack are old friends.

Jack frowns. "I'm not sure I like this."

"Second thoughts, Jack?" Alexei asks with a grin.

That has Jack pausing. He may not be happy about how this is going, but he's not ready to back out. "I have questions."

"Of course you do," Alexei announces with way too much cheer. "That's why we're here."

He walks to the front door and scans his pass. The door silently slides open and Alexei enters, assuming Jack's following.

Which is exactly what Jack does, wondering how Alexei even has a pass. He's not FBI, he's NASA.

Whistling again, Alexei makes his way to the elevator and Jack has little choice but to follow. What's worse, he wants to follow. He realizes the moment Alexei said the word "Nebula" he was already invested.

Inside the elevator, Alexei swipes his pass again. He looks at Jack as he stands beside him and winks. Jack looks away, staring straight ahead. Alexei is getting on his nerves.

They start descending and Jack tenses. They're headed for the parking lot. It will be practically deserted this time of night. No witnesses if Jack has just stupidly walked straight into a trap.

The lights on the control panel flash as they head below ground. One floor. Two floors. Three floors. With each one, Jack's hand creeps closer to his gun. He won't be going down without a fight.

And getting some answers.

The elevator dings as they reach the final floor. Seven levels of nothing but solid concrete are above them.

But the elevator doesn't stop. To Jack's amazement, it continues its downward path, despite the fact there are no more floors.

Except, apparently there are.

Alexei grins. "Pretty cool, huh? Right under your nose the whole time!"

A few moments later, the elevator stops. Jack's guessing they're about ten floors beneath ground level.

The doors open and he braces himself, not sure what he's expecting. But all that greets him are two more large doors, bare concrete on either side illuminated by fluorescent lighting. Alexei steps out and stops in front of the doors, looking over his shoulder at Jack, looking like a child who's about to share Santa's toy room.

Jack follows. Bare corridors stretch out both left and right, and he notes the closed doors lining both sides.

"Ready?" Alexei asks.

"I'm guessing it's too late if I'm not." This place is obviously top secret. Jack doubts many people know of its existence.

Alexei chuckles. "Yep. We'd have to kill you."

Pushing open the doors like he didn't just casually threaten an FBI agent, Alexei enters the room. Jack stays where he is, taking in what he's seeing.

An area that looks like a NASA control room is stretched out before him. Rows of computers, some alive with numbers rolling down their screens, some black and asleep, are everywhere. But what captures Jack's attention and doesn't let go is the massive movie-screen sized image projected on the far wall.

"That's the asteroid, isn't it?"

Alexei walks in further, nodding as he looks at the image of the monstrous rock hurtling through space. "That's her, all right."

Jack enters, his feet moving of their own volition. Enveloped by the hum of the computers, he barely glances at his surroundings. He's already noted the place is stark. Empty of people except for them. And well funded.

But seeing the asteroid as if it's so close has him entranced. "I didn't know we could see it in such detail."

"Nebula has technology most people only dream about."

Jack narrows his eyes as he processes what that means. "Then what do you know about it?"

Alexei scratches his whiskery chin, his eyes lighting up like that was the right question to ask. "Well, this one appeared out of nowhere. And there's been strange fluctuations at the place the asteroid first appeared. I keep telling them it's changes in dark matter but, seeing as we can't see it or measure it, it keeps being relegated as a theory."

"We?"

The whisker scratching intensifies, like Alexei's getting excited. "Nebula. Our job is to keep an eye out there"—he points to the image of space—"for, well, anything."

Jack tears his gaze away from the asteroid that feels like it's growing in size by the second so he can pin Alexei with his gaze. "Who do you work for?"

"The Director."

Jack waits but Alexei doesn't elaborate. "That's it? The Director?"

Alexei shrugs. "That's as much as anyone knows. They head a top-secret organization, after all."

Frowning, Jack files that away for future reference. Right now, one question is waiting—burning—to be asked.

"So, we're not alone?"

Alexei snorts. "Just our galaxy is estimated to be home to at least one hundred billion planets. Of course we're not alone." He rubs his hands together. "The real question is, are the others friend or foe? And are they here?"

Jack mulls over this. Can they really afford to wait and find out?

"And you want me to join you in this search?"

Alexei opens his arms out wide. "You already have, Jack."

Opening his mouth to respond, Jack slams it shut again. He doubts Alexei was joking when he said they'd have to kill him if he refuses. They can't afford for someone to leak any knowledge of Nebula's existence.

Not that it matters. Jack's career has been working toward this moment. The discovery that he's not alone in his beliefs.

And proof that Earth isn't alone, either.

Jack enters the room more fully, leaning his hands on the

back of a chair in the center of the room. "So, what's the plan?"

Alexei grins "First of all, we need to nuke the asteroid. The coordinates for the missile have been calculated—just a few millimetres off and we'll miss, or whack it into Saturn or something. Then, we figure out where this sucker came from." Alexei wiggles his brows. "Which is where you come in, Agent Cadbury. We're hoping your extensive research may have generated a lead or two."

A stillness settles over Jack. A calmness he hasn't felt in a long time. Even his ulcers go quiet for this moment. He smiles as two words float through his mind.

Tristan. Ayers.

28

CASSANDRA

Cassandra checks her watch. Five minutes to noon. In just a few hours, every news station on the planet will be sharing the broadcast of NASA's missile launch.

The last few days have been insane. Every grocery store and fast food joint in the area has been hit by apparently stupid people who believe the rumors about the Oreos. Honestly, if anything other than money should become the new world currency, it should be cleansing wipes. Any challenge can be faced with clear skin and tight pores, and she's certain the world will soon realize their value and start hoarding them just like she did when she hid hers under a floorboard in her closet.

All schools have been closed until further notice, which basically means until the world sees how the missile will pan out. Cassandra never imagined she would miss school so much. She's tried to see her friends as much as possible, but aside from the other Zodiacs, everyone is hunkering down with their families. Even Suki, who hates her little brother, has been making excuses to stay home. She even posted a picture on Insta of the two of them playing Sorry.

Meanwhile, Cassandra's hardly left her room all the time she's been at home. But she can't avoid it any longer. Her stomach is starting to growl, and she's always found that sound utterly disgusting. Conceding to her finely toned musculature's constant need for protein, she reluctantly opens her door and ventures into the kitchen.

"No, that is unacceptable!" her mother yells into her phone, her shrill voice carrying from the living room. "The order was supposed to be here *today* and I expect it *today*!"

Cassandra grabs a handful of protein bars from the cabinet. These should do. Although, she's very thirsty, too. Maybe a juice from the fridge...

"Ugh, how ridiculous!" Her mother storms into the kitchen and slams her phone on the counter.

Crap, not fast enough.

"Can you believe this?" her mother whines.

"What?" Cassandra asks only because she has to.

"Costco claims they're completely sold out of toilet paper! When I placed the order, their website said no such thing." She points her finger indignantly to further state her claim. "Now what are we going to do? All the stores are empty, too."

"We have several dozen rolls, I think we'll be fine," Cassandra points out.

"Yes, but how long will those last us with the rest of the world going crazy?" Her mother flaps her hands around wildly as she speaks. She's the epitome of hysterical right now. "I refuse to resort to using leaves." Her botoxed lips actually twist in a disgusted frown, which is an impressive feat.

"Don't be silly." Cassandra waves a faux reassuring hand. "We'll go through all the coffee filters before that happens."

Her mother scowls at her. "I do not need your sass right now, young lady." She places both hands on the counter and hangs her head, making a weeping sound. "Why is this happening to me?"

This is happening to all of us, Cassandra thinks with disdain.

All of her friends' parents are doing all they can to comfort their kids, and here's Cassandra's mother, worrying only about her own hardships, which aren't even as big as those of most.

But, she is Cassandra's mother, after all. Maybe Cassandra isn't doing enough to comfort her?

Cassandra moves closer and puts her hand on her mom's shoulder. "I'm sure that all the factories are rushing to create more. Toilet paper will be back in stock in no time, and no doubt your order will be the first to be filled."

Her mother lifts her head and looks at her with moist eyes. "You really think so?"

Cassandra offers a smile. "Of course."

Her mom suddenly throws her arms around Cassandra, catching Cassandra off guard. "Oh, I hope so."

Sighing and rolling her eyes with an accepting smile, Cassandra pats her mother's back. Maybe now that she's coaxed her mom into a state of slightly less hysterics, she can escape back to her room until it's time to head to Tristan's.

No sooner as she and her mom withdraw from the very rare embrace, the front door closes, which can only mean one thing.

Her father is home.

Oh, no.

"Ah, well don't you girls look cozy," he says as he enters the kitchen, wearing his I-just-made-a-deal smile.

"Oh, dear, you won't believe this," her mother says as she turns to him, right back to her full hysterics. "Costco cancelled our toilet paper delivery, claiming they're out of stock!"

He comes closer and pecks her on the cheek. "Don't you worry about that, darling. Business never stops, not even times like these. In fact, it only gets better! They'll be back in stock in no time and I can assure you that we'll be the first delivery."

"That's what Cassandra said." Her mother wipes away a tear before it can be seen.

"Well, even a broken clock is right twice a day," he says as he brushes past Cassandra without a look.

Cassandra's palms instinctively warm, and all she can do is clench them, deepening the scars from her fingernails.

"You look quite pleased," her mother points out as Cassandra attempts to escape unnoticed.

"I am, indeed!" he declares, pulling a bottle of port from the liquor cabinet and pouring it into a fine crystal glass. "Like I said, business thrives during times of panic."

That has Cassandra stopping in her tracks. She knows better. She knows she should just keep walking, avoid as much confrontation with her dad as possible.

But she can't. Not this time.

She turns. "What do you mean?"

He takes a sip and savors the liquid as he regards her with disdain. "I think it's time I teach you a valuable life lesson, Cassandra. You see, in times of uncertainty, people panic. Businesses go belly up. Properties get sold for nothing. And the wisest of us can benefit greatly from the stupidity of others."

She swallows back all the vile things she's thinking about his business dealings and feigns ignorance. "How so?"

"Well, Pierce Financing just finalized their deal with us with far less haggling than I'd hoped," he says proudly. "Not to mention, I bought another company for pennies on the dollar. Once all this madness dies down, we'll be making more money than ever.."

Cassandra's blood boils, knowing that Brielle's parents are the ones who will suffer the most from this. But she doesn't let that knowledge show on her face.

"So, you really don't think there's anything to worry about, with this asteroid on a collision course for the moon?"

He swallows another sip and hisses through his teeth before answering. "Not at all! The people at NASA are fellow brilliant businessmen. I have no doubt they will put an end to this crisis, and the world will return to business as usual. And when it does, we will prosper."

The heat in her clenched fists increases. "And what if the missile fails and the moon is destroyed?"

He laughs as if she's just said something foolish and puts his glass down with a decisive *clink*. "That won't happen."

"But what if it does?" She's heard about Tristan's visions. He saw both scenarios, one where the missile hits the asteroid, and one where the asteroid strikes the moon, and all is lost. Cassandra isn't one to bet on the better outcome.

Her father's face turns to steel, a scowl etched into his brow. "If it does, we will still come out on top. We will hold all the wealth, and the injured and poor will turn to us for guidance, which we will gladly offer, for a price."

Her anger is at a boiling point, and she's not sure she can stand much more of this. Taking his beatings, that she could do, but she can't stand idly by while he ruins the lives of others.

She's been a fool all this time. Siding with him, believing he had a good side, fighting for that good side, and withstanding the punishment for doing so with silence. No longer.

"And if all currency goes belly up, and your wealth means nothing, what then?" She flares a daring eyebrow at him.

His scowl deepens, and she can all but feel his anger

radiate across the few feet that separate them. "Cassandra, I think you and I need to have a private word in my office."

She knows what that means, but with her mother standing here, she has an out.

"Actually, I have a prior *business* engagement," she says with a bravado she never knew she had. "We can reconvene later."

With that, she turns on her heel and goes straight out the door. She hardly cares that she just completely snubbed her father. There's a fifty-fifty chance none of them will live to see tomorrow anyway.

At least she can say she went out swinging.

29

TRISTAN

The tension in HQ is so thick, Tristan's pretty sure he could use it for resistance training. Every TV screen and computer monitor is alive, filled with images of reporters, the asteroid, or the missile that's being prepared for launch.

But they're all mute, bar one. Tristan stands beside Brielle, the other Zodiacs and Veronica clustered around, as they watch the largest screen up on the wall.

It's Dr. Alexei Antonov's round, whiskered face that has everyone's rapt attention. He's sitting across from Sofia, the news anchor, as she smiles at him, no doubt because her channel scored this exclusive interview. Behind them is the live broadcast from NASA.

Only viewed from a distance, where hundreds of TV vans are parked, the site is largely bare apart from a gray, squat building in the center.

Oh, and the large, black missile locked into place beside it, pointing for the sky.

Sofia smiles at the camera and Tristan admires her cool.

The calm-faced, steady-handed persona she's presenting is just what the world needs at the moment.

Because inside, everyone—including Sofia—is terrified right now.

She turns back to Alexei. "It looks like they're making the final preparations," she observes.

"They most certainly are," Alexei responds with his out-of-place cheer. "As you know, there were a lot of careful, considered calculations made. The size of the missile—we want to destroy this asteroid, but not take out half the galaxy. And then there's the trajectory. The missile has to hit the asteroid at its core for it to be destroyed."

Sofia's perfectly plucked brows twitch a little closer together. "And if it doesn't?"

"It won't miss. That's why we spent so long triangulating the data."

"Although—"

Alexei leans forward. "Sofia, Sofia, Sofia. I, personally, oversaw said calculations. Rest assured, we're about to watch an indisputable moment in history."

Sofia presses her hand to her ear as she glances at the screen. Turning, she straightens her shoulders. "We've just received word they're about to commence the launch sequence."

Brielle shifts her weight uneasily, and Tristan finds himself instinctively moving a little closer. If only things were different...

Sofia's hand goes to her ear again. Her face settles into calm lines as she stares directly into the camera. "The launch sequence has begun."

The image behind Sofia enlarges, engulfing the screen. The missile, black and sleek, becomes the focal point.

A disembodied voice crackles through HQ. "Fire in the launch."

Veronica tucks into Jareth's side. He wraps his arms around her, holding her tightly.

"Ten."

Cassandra frowns as she chews on a painted nail.

"Nine. Eight."

Tristan glances at Brielle, conscious that the small distance between them feels too far. He tells himself it shouldn't...but it still does. She turns to him as if she could sense his gaze, flickers an almost sad smile, and turns back to the screen.

"Four. Three."

Brielle's stopped breathing. Tristan's own chest feels like it's about to collapse under the pressure in the room. Without thinking, his hand reaches out, finding Brielle's waiting for him. Their hands clasp, fingers entwining. Tristan doesn't tear his gaze away from the screen, but something in him calms. Like his blood pressure just went down. Like he remembered that this could all be okay.

"Two. One. Lift off."

Fire mushrooms out from beneath the missile, billowing in every direction, almost looking like it's engulfing the missile itself. Jareth leans forward as it feels like time slows. All that's visible is the tip of the missile, a tumbling mass of flames multiplying and growing as they scorch everything in its path.

Memories of Jareth's house fire flicker through Tristan's mind. Flashes of the barren, ash-covered wasteland that was left behind.

It never occurred to him that the missile could end up with the same fate.

A blaze of light explodes at the base of the missile, as bright as the sun, and it powers into the sky. It spears straight up and into the clouds, a shooting star leaving a thick column of smoke in its wake.

Within seconds, it's gone. Its path programmed for the asteroid. For destruction.

Realizing he's holding Brielle's hand, Tristan quickly releases it. They were supporting each other as friends, nothing else.

"That was…impressive," he mutters.

"It had better do the job," says Cassandra, her tone just as grim.

The image minimizes and Alexei and Sofia appear again. Alexei leans back like a satisfied businessman. "Textbook launch. Everything's going according to plan."

"That's wonderful news," Sofia says with relief. "How is NASA tracking the missile's progress?"

"That missile is using some of the most advanced technology we have. It will be streaming live data, although that will take a few minutes to reach us. Then we can give the all-clear," Alexei beams. He leans forward, winking at Sofia. "Although I'm going to be a little disappointed that Oreos will no longer become a new world currency."

Tristan snorts as he shakes his head. He can't believe that was actually going to be a thing.

Suddenly, one of the smaller TV screens to the right flashes and flickers. The Zodiacs frown at each other, wondering what's going on.

The screen goes black and quickly comes back to life, this time, filled with an image of space.

"Holy pitch," breathes Tristan.

A missile is streaking across the blackness. The asteroid is approaching it from the other end of the screen.

Veronica leans closer. "You guys can tap into satellite images?"

"Not that we knew of," says Tristan. He looks around the room, impressed to a whole new level. "Alden, you genius."

Brielle's wide-eyed as she takes in the collision course.

"Alden must be scanning space. Looks like he can tap into satellite feeds."

Jareth's eyes narrow. "NASA would be watching this."

"In real time," adds Veronica.

Which means Alexei hasn't told Sofia the entire truth. NASA doesn't want the rest of the world to watch this.

The missile continues its arrow-like trajectory, and the closer it comes to the asteroid, the larger the picture becomes.

Tristan lets out a low whistle. "They can zoom that sucker in."

Cassandra's back to chewing her fake nail. "That's one heck of an asteroid."

She's right. The spiraling mass of rock is so much bigger than Tristan expected. Which would be why Alexei called it a planetoid.

"The missile will take care of it," says Brielle quietly.

Tristan tears his gaze away to flash her a quick smile. Brielle's always the voice of faith and optimism. No wonder he's so drawn to her.

When he looks back, the distance between the missile and asteroid has all but disappeared. Millions of miles dissolve as the two power toward each other.

Tristan braces himself for the impact, as if he's going to feel the massive explosion from here.

The tip of the missile spears into the asteroid.

Tristan steps closer to the TV. "That didn't look like the center—"

The missile crumples and explodes. Fire, debris and rock fragments blast outward, filling the image with dust and flames.

"Did it work?" Brielle asks in a half-whisper.

They have to wait for breathless seconds for the aftermath of the explosion to clear. When it does, the Zodiacs rear back.

The missile is gone, shards of metal spinning through the vacuum of space. But the asteroid is still there, and it's changed trajectory.

Now, it's coming straight for the satellite. Straight for them.

"No." Tristan almost moans the word.

Sofia's voice ruptures the silence that's descended in HQ. She's facing the replay image of the missile launch. "According to my calculations, the missile should've hit the asteroid by now, Alexei?"

Sofia turns back, only to find the other side of the desk empty.

Alexei's gone.

She looks around in confusion, only to suddenly stop as her hand returns to her ear. Sofia's eyes widen, her hand sliding back down like her arm just lost all its strength. For some reason, Tristan no longer wishes he was still holding Brielle's hand.

He wishes he was holding all of her.

So pale even her lips lose their color beneath her lipstick, Sofia blinks. "The missile did not destroy the asteroid. It has now changed trajectory." Swallowing visibly, Sofia speaks again, her voice little more than a whisper. "The asteroid is now Earthbound."

30

BRIELLE

This can't be happening. This can't be happening!

"This can't be happening," she whispers aloud.

The four of them sit in HQ, silent and utterly stunned. The grim look on Tristan's face mirrors the horror that floods every inch of her.

The missile hit the asteroid wrong. The asteroid is now heading for Earth. Their planet will be hit in mere hours.

What are they going to do? How can they do anything? They're just four humans—albeit humans with superpowers, but of the four of them, only two have powers that can actually inflict damage. All Tristan can do is see the future, two variations of which he can never discern the truth. And Brielle. Her lie-detection is useless against the asteroid—as with most other threats. Seriously, she drew the short draw in the power raffle. She's useless against Skins, useless against Chardis's attacks. She's only good against Chardis himself, who's all but disappeared since their first meeting. He'd much rather stick to the shadows and attack them from afar, which is how he'll win.

This will be Chardis's ultimate victory. He's going to take

out all thirteen Zodiac Guardians in one fell swoop. Unless they can stop it.

But how?

Tristan turns to her, and she swears she can see the same desire burning in his eyes that she did the other night. It's all she can do not to wrap her arms around him. Maybe she should. If the world ends today, what difference would it make?

"What are we going to do?" It's Cassandra's voice that breaks the solemn silence.

Tristan severs the long-suffering glance with Brielle and looks at Cassandra. He shakes his head, looking utterly defeated. "I…I don't know."

"We have to do something," Jareth says, cupping his chin in deliberation. "That asteroid will hit in just a few hours." His dark eyes dart back and forth as he ponders. "Maybe I can create a missile of our own and shoot it at the asteroid."

Tristan sighs loudly, hanging his head. "Even if we did, there's no guarantee we'd hit our mark. NASA has the world's best mathematicians and scientists, and even they missed." He shakes his head again. "No, if we were to do that, we'd have to be right in front of the missile."

Brielle gasps, understanding the impossible meaning of his words. "As in, *go* to the missile?"

Cassandra's pacing like a hungry lioness in Brielle's peripheral vision, but Brielle is so emotionally lost herself that she can't offer support.

Jareth leans forward in his chair, frowning deeply. "Is that even possible?"

The two look at Tristan, who's a perfect statue in his seat, unmoving even to breathe. It seems an eternity before he finally moves enough to speak. "I can't say for certain, but I have to imagine that our suits are built to withstand space travel. We already know they can fly, and they're air tight, so they must have an oxygenation system, which is all we really need to go into space." He's silent again as his eyes play ping pong in his head, considering. "Our forebearers were defenders of galaxies, with many of their battles taking place in space. So our suits must be able to withstand the circumstances of a vacuum."

"Is that something you're willing to bet our lives on?" Jareth asks.

Tristan raises grim eyes to meet his. "What choice do we have?"

"I need some air," Cassandra says, then rushes out of the room.

Feeling a little clouded herself, Brielle races after her. They need Cassandra right now.

Brielle needs her.

She enters the hallway to find Cassandra pacing once more, chewing on her fingernails.

"Cassandra?" Brielle asks, ready to offer what comfort she can, even though she knows reassurance went out the window with the missile.

Cassandra suddenly stops and throws her hands up. "This can't be it!" she yells. "He can't win, just like that!"

"It's not the end," Brielle says with conviction. She couldn't have said it if she didn't believe it. "We'll figure out a solution, and we'll come out on top. I just know it."

Cassandra turns outraged golden eyes on her. "What about Tristan's visions? He said that either the missile would hit the asteroid or it would miss and the asteroid would destroy the moon!"

Brielle swallows, understanding the confusion. "The missile did hit. But Tristan couldn't have known that would mean the asteroid would veer off course toward Earth."

"So what then? Our powers are just completely useless?"

Cassandra looks every bit the lion, and Brielle realizes how fitting her Zodiac sign truly is, has always been.

"No. They're not useless." Brielle looks down, trying to find the right words, even though she's always thought her own powers to be exactly that. "We each play a vital role in this team. And it's only as a team that we'll solve this current predicament."

Cassandra shakes her and resumes pacing, her hands glowing slightly in the dim hallway.

"Please, come back inside, and we'll decide on a plan," Brielle urges, the need to be by Tristan's side overpowering. Like an itch she's powerless not to scratch.

Abruptly, Cassandra stops and pulls out her phone, staring at it for a long moment.

"I need to call my parents," she says, eyes fixed on the screen.

Brielle freezes, completely bewildered.

When she says nothing, Cassandra disappears down the hall.

Leaving Brielle standing in the hallway alone.

She remains in the half-lit stillness, just outside of the room where the one person she adores most is struggling without her.

But she can't shake this most out of place feeling.

It doesn't make sense. Brielle ponders it for a moment, torn between following Cassandra and going back to help Tristan formulate a plan.

Cassandra lied.

JACK

13:37

"This isn't open to argument, Veronica," Jack growls into his cell. "I want you here, now."

There's a pause on the other end. "Okay," his daughter says tearfully. "I just need to say goodbye to Jareth."

Jack lets out a pent up breath. "I told you he can come, too."

Veronica had tried insisting she'll be safer at her friend's house, adamant that it was the equivalent of a bunker. But Veronica doesn't know Nebula exists. That they have offices deep in the bowels of New York.

And that they're the safest place she can be.

"And I told you he won't come," Veronica retorts, some of her usual sass coming back. "He has things he has to take care of."

"Don't we all," mutters Jack. "Look, the offer's there if he changes his mind. Right now, I need to know you're going to be safe."

Veronica sighs. "I'll be there in about half an hour."

They hang up, and Jack looks around the empty FBI offices. With the asteroid on a trajectory for Earth, everyone's gone home. They have more important things to think of. Like survival.

Jack rattles a couple of antacids into his palm, wondering what he'll do when he runs out. So many things are about to become things of the past. Medication. Homes. Normality.

His cell rings and Jack picks it up, seeing that it's Clara. At least it's not Logan telling him he's going to be late. Having both of his children here is Jack's only priority right now.

"Hey, what's up?"

"I have some news."

"Now?" What could Clara have to tell him that could be that important?

"I thought you might want to know that McNally's dead. They found his body in the abandoned apartment building."

Jack slumps back in his chair. "Well, there you go…"

"He'd been thrown onto the pile of timbers and one of them punctured his chest. Any ideas of who could've done it?"

Tristan. Which means Tristan has taken care of their common foe. This truce may have been a good idea, after all.

Jack clears his throat. Jack isn't saying any of that to Clara. "I'd have to look at the crime scene—"

"Bullshit, Jack. You know more than you're letting on."

Jack sits up, a little shocked. "Of course we all have theories, Clara, but—"

"There are too many parts to this puzzle that don't match up. You think this has to do with the Zodiac Heirs, don't you?"

Jack doesn't say anything as he tries to come up with a suitable response. He can't say that he *knows* this has to do with the Zodiac Heirs. His next step is to find out what they are, and how they're connected to everything that's happening.

Clara speaks into the pause, her voice low. "You think this has to do with aliens, don't you?"

Frowning, Jack wonders if his drop-kick boss, Flanagan, has got in her ear. "Who have you been talking to?"

"I believe you, Jack," she blurts. "I know there's more out there. It's why I asked to be partnered with you."

Jack hesitates. Someone else who believes him. Could Clara be a potential recruit for Nebula?

Jack glances at his watch. Another half an hour or so and his kids will be here. Now's not the time to be making decisions like this. "Look, Clara, I don't have time to talk about this right now. Let's—"

"Well, that's disappointing," she states flatly and hangs up.

Jack looks at his cell phone, confused.

"Is it the Klingons?" Alexei jokes from the door. "They can say some pretty weird stuff sometimes."

Jack puts his cell down, shaking his head. "I'll be down shortly. I'm just waiting for Logan and Veronica."

Alexei scratches his whiskers. "And you're sure we can trust them?"

"They're my kids, of course I can trust them."

"Jack. The Director himself wanted you recruited. You're a top notch investigator who's realized there's far more to this world than our little planet." Alexei raises his brows. "Don't let personal feelings cloud your judgment."

Frowning, Jack jams his cell into his pocket. "I'd trust them with my life," he growls.

Alexei pulls up a megawatt smile. "That's great, then. I look forward to meeting them."

The sound of footsteps has them both turning around. Jack expects Veronica to come striding in, still annoyed that she was torn away from her beloved boyfriend, but Jack's surprised to see Clara entering the room.

She takes note of Alexei standing next to Jack, her face unsmiling.

"Clara," says Jack. "I said we can't have this conversation right now."

Clara snorts then reaches behind her back and pulls out a gun. "I think we should."

Alexei's hands shoot up in the air. "Whoa! If this is a lovers' tiff—"

"Shut up," snaps Clara. "Jack is a man of principles, of integrity," she says, practically spitting the words out. She angles her head. "Although, I think I was wearing you down."

Jack's mind is working overtime as he tries to figure out what's going on. "You actually were," he concedes, not liking that it's the truth. "How about we put the gun down and talk about whatever's going on here?"

In response, Clara lifts the pistol and aims it more squarely at his chest. "You've been keeping secrets, Jack."

Alexei takes a step forward. "Look, I'm sure we can work this out—"

"Shut up," Clara snaps again, not taking her gaze off Jack. "Where did the two of you go when you entered this building the other night?"

Clara was following him. Watching.

"I searched every damned floor."

"Secret men's bathroom," Alexei jokes, even adding a wink for good measure. "It was time Jack knew about it."

"Shut. Up," Clara growls, her gaze flicking toward Alexei. "You have no importance to me."

The threat in her tone is unmistakable and Jack realizes this is serious. Deadly serious.

"None of you have have figured it out." Clara's gaze blazes triumphantly. "We're everywhere."

"We," Alexei breathes under his breath, putting Jack's teeth on edge. Doesn't he realize that Clara means business?

She takes a step forward, the gun unerringly pointed at Jack's heart. "I was the one who helped McNally escape. He promised all he needed was a second chance." She curls her lip in distaste. "And the Zodiacs killed him."

This perks Alexei up. "Did you say Zodiacs?"

Jack flashes him a warning frown, but Alexei does what he least expects. He winks at him.

Jack's gaze shoots back to Clara as he realizes Alexei is doing this on purpose.

He's trying to distract her. Keep her talking.

He must realize Jack has his gun in his holster. He's

waiting for the right moment, a little part of him was hoping that Clara was just bluffing.

But her cold features are hard with intent. She's here to kill.

"Who are you?" Jack asks, part-furious, part conscious that he's in mortal danger.

"Once I'm done with you—you were getting too close to the truth, by the way—then I'll take care of Tristan and the other Zodiacs."

Tristan. The Zodiacs. Jack should've known this was all related.

Clara narrows her eyes. "We thought you could be useful, Jack."

And the fool that he is, he even fleetingly considered showing Clara Nebula. His hand twitches, knowing Clara has the advantage. Her firearm is already out and aimed at her target.

Jack.

"We?" Alexei asks.

"But we were disappointed."

"There's the 'we' again. Who do you work for?"

Clara never takes her eyes off Jack as her arm swings out, pulls the trigger, and shoots Alexei in the chest.

Except the moment she moves, a second shot rings out. Clara's body jerks with the impact of the bullet Jack just fired, her eyes flying wide open then fluttering closed as her body crumples to the ground.

Jack waits for the space of a breath to make sure she's not getting up again, then rushes to Alexei. He stands over the man's still body, seeing that he doesn't need to check for a pulse to know he's dead. The stain of the bullet wound is blooming exactly where Alexei's heart would be. The poor guy died too young.

Breathing hard although he's barely moved, Jack looks

around the office, trying to process what just happened. Clara was a spy, but for which organization, he doesn't know. Alexei is dead. And someone wants the Zodiacs just as much as he does.

Jack reaches for his antacids. He needs to meet Logan and Veronica at the door. They don't need to see two dead bodies only hours before the asteroid is slated to hit Earth.

Jack's taken two steps when his cell rings. He answers it without looking at the screen, assuming it's one of his children. He needs to tell them not to come in here.

Except it's not Logan's voice who reaches his ear. Or Veronica's.

"Hey Jack, it's Alexei here. If you're receiving this prerecorded message, then I'm dead. The only way this call could've been triggered is because the sensor I implanted in my chest is no longer registering a heartbeat, which sucks on more than one level to be perfectly honest. Not only will I never get to ask Sofia out on a date, Nebula is now leaderless."

Jack looks at his cell, then at Alexei's dead body, shocked at the surrealness of what's happening. Alexei was the Director? And he's contacting him before his body has even had a chance to go cold?

"Anywho, I just wanted to let you know, I appoint you as my successor. You are now the Director of Nebula."

There's silence and Jack blinks, assuming the message is finished. Except there's a soft sound, almost like a scratching of whiskers, and then Alexei speaks again.

"I have one piece of advice in this fight to save Earth. Choose your recruits carefully, just like I did."

31

JARETH

Jareth hunches around his phone, trying to get what privacy he can in HQ. "Hey, I just wanted to check you got to your Dad okay."

"Hey," Veronica answers, her voice husky with the knowledge that neither of them wishes they were apart right now. "Yeah, although he's acting all weird."

Jareth feels like he hasn't stopped frowning since the moment the news anchor announced the new trajectory of the asteroid. But now, his brows sink even deeper. Watching Veronica leave was one of the hardest things he's ever done.

But he assumed she'd be safe with Jack.

"Weird how?" he asks tensely.

"I'm not sure. He was waiting for me outside the building when I got here. And now we're still out here, waiting for Logan."

"You all need to be inside."

There's an asteroid heading for Earth, for pitch sake!

"That's what I tried to tell him," Veronica says, and Jareth can just imagine she's rolling her eyes. "But something's got him rattled, so I'm not pushing it."

Jareth sighs. "Everyone's rattled."

"So..." Veronica's voice has become hushed and a little muffled, like she has the cell closer to her mouth. "What are you guys planning?"

Rubbing his forehead, Jareth glances over his shoulder. Tristan and Brielle are talking, probably unaware of how close together they're standing. They always seem to gravitate toward each other when things get tough. He looks around again, noting he can't see Cassandra. Only a few moments ago she was pacing like a caged lion, every now and again flexing her shoulders as if she was squaring up for a fight.

Which is exactly what they're doing.

"We're going to go on up there and nuke the asteroid."

Although he says the words as calmly as he can, Jareth's heart flutters at the thought of what they have to do. Fly into space. Obliterate the asteroid. Return to Earth unseen.

Veronica whistles under her breath. "I had a feeling you'd say something like that."

"Right now, it's our only hope."

"That Chardis is an asshat," Veronica spits angrily. She pauses. "I wish I was there..."

Jareth's hand tightens around his cell. "I know. Me, too." He'd be holding her right now, reassuring her just as much as himself that this is all going to work out. "But you had to be with your dad."

"I should also be with you," she says miserably.

Jareth's chest constricts. Being torn between the Zodiacs and her father is something Veronica constantly has to deal with. She loves Jack, and yet she has to betray him each time he asks about the Zodiacs. What's more, she relays everything she knows, allowing them to stay one step ahead of the one man who wants their identities known—her father.

And yet, as Earth faces a disaster of epic proportions, she

should be with her family. They need her more than the Zodiacs do.

Although, not more than Jareth does.

"You've still got the daisy?" he asks.

"Of course I do," she huffs. "I love you, Jareth," she adds, her voice softening. "I'll take any connection to you I can get."

Jareth's eyes slam closed. "I love you, too. And we don't need a daisy to be connected."

Jareth and Veronica are connected at the heart. Their souls.

The sound of something crashing to the ground has Jareth spinning around. He sees Tristan straighten after he must've staggered.

Brielle's hands flutter out to reach him. "Tristan, is everything okay?"

But Tristan doesn't answer. He goes ramrod straight, staring ahead like he's just fallen into a trance.

"Jareth! I think he's having another vision!"

"I've gotta go, Veronica," he says into the phone. "Tristan's being more weird than usual."

"Keep me posted," she asks quickly before Jareth hangs up. He rushes over to Tristan, who's still unmoving.

Brielle's face is tight with concern. "It must be a vision."

Tristan jerks once, twice, then stills again, his breath coming in gasps. Jareth watches, worry gripping his gut like a vice, as Tristan's sightless eyes widen, his face twisting with grief.

"I wonder what he's seeing," whispers Brielle.

Jareth doesn't answer. Whatever it is, it doesn't look good.

Seconds later, Tristan stumbles forward and Brielle catches him. Jareth quickly helps her to get Tristan into a chair.

He hangs his head in his hands for long moments, getting his breathing under control. Brielle and Jareth wait, tense at the thought of what they're about to learn.

When Tristan looks up, his face is the palest Jareth's ever seen. "I saw the asteroid."

Brielle and Jareth glance at each other, then wait again. Tristan always has two visions. Two alternate realities that could play out.

And one will.

"In the first, the asteroid is destroyed. Obliterated to smithereens. I'm not sure how, but I think Cassandra's there. There's a lot of light."

"Well, that's good news," murmurs Brielle, her face trying to look encouraging.

Tristan's eyes close as he draws in a deep breath. When he opens them, it's clear that the second vision doesn't end as well.

"In the second, the asteroid is heading to Earth." He swallows, seeming to find it hard to hold eye contact. "It shoots straight past Cassandra's lifeless body. Nothing stops it."

"Oh, Tristan," Brielle breathes, her voice full of the horror that Tristan just witnessed.

Cassandra dead. Earth destroyed. Everything lost.

Brielle straightens. "We're going to have to make sure the first vision is the right one then, won't we?"

Tristan nods, a little color returning to his face. "Yeah, you're right. That's exactly what we're going to have to do."

Clinging to the hope the two of them just created, Jareth looks around. The only movement in HQ is the images flickering on the many monitors, documenting the chaos raining down on every inch of the globe.

Tristan shoots to his feet. "Cassandra? Cassandra!"

They wait in breathless limbo, straining to hear a

response. Jareth's heart thuds heavily in his chest, feeling like a harbinger of doom.

There's no answer.

HQ is empty apart from the three of them.

Cassandra's gone.

32

CASSANDRA

S he has to move quickly. She's sure that Brielle sensed she was lying.

But Cassandra had to.

She's lived her life pretty selfishly. This is her chance to make up for all the times she spread rumors about her peers, made fun of someone, actively worked to make someone miserable—like she has with Brielle for a decade. She already put Brielle's life at risk once. Cassandra's not going to let her get this close to danger.

Cassandra knows she can do this on her own. The other Zodiacs certainly can't. Brielle and Tristan's powers are metaphysical, they can't defend against the massive hunk of rock determined to destroy the planet. And what's Jareth going to do? Throw imagined balloons at it?

No, she knows with every fiber of her being that she's the only one who can do this. She's going to save the world, right now.

I'm going to prove that my father is wrong, and that he always has been. I'm a hero. I am not a disappointment!

Cassandra walks briskly around the corner and down

into the alleyway of Tristan's neighborhood. Even with the imminent threat of impact, she can't risk exposing herself. In a few hours, she'll obliterate the asteroid and the world will be safe, and everything will go back to normal. No reason to out the Zodiacs over something that is just a scare.

Once she's found a location that offers enough privacy, she grips the yellow tanzanite hanging around her neck and says the word Tristan taught her.

"Akash."

The sexy golden suit envelopes her from head to toe, and she feels more powerful than she's ever felt. This is her moment. This is what she was always destined for.

Without a clue as to how to fly—Tristan hasn't taught her that yet—she bends her knees and kicks off the ground, half expecting to come right back down.

But she doesn't.

With all the momentum of her forceful leap, she shoots upward into the air. Exhilaration floods her veins with electric heat as she watches the ground fall away from her more and more quickly.

It worked! She's actually flying!

With a victorious smile exploding across her face, she straightens her body, imitating a rocket, which allows her to cut even faster through the clouds. Higher and higher she soars, the pale blue of the sky around her growing rapidly darker until it fades away completely to star-spangled black.

A sense of awe—and a hint of fear—momentarily paralyzes her within her rocketing suit. She's in freaking space! Will she even be able to breathe? How long will the air inside this suit last? And the fact that there are no surfaces anywhere, no land, no solid ground to step on or grab onto, tightens her chest with sudden agoraphobia.

Her breathing quickens, her pulse speeding. She has to calm down.

Breathe. Stay in control.

She closes her eyes, clenches her fists, and forces herself to take long, heavy breaths.

Stay calm. You're in control.

Her breathing slows, and her heart no longer feels like it's trying to burst out of her chest.

She opens her eyes, and the confident grin returns to her face. "Okay, time to save the world."

Turning her head all around, she looks for the asteroid. All she sees in every direction is glittery black. She spins around, and the sudden brightness of the sun forces her to shield her eyes.

Probably not that way.

She blinks away the green stains in her vision, looking down. Earth is breathtaking. A seemingly endless expanse of green-brown land surrounded by blue of every shade and tone. She can make out the shape of the United States below her. Everyone she knows and loves is down there, depending on her.

Cassandra raises her head, returning to her search.

How can it be this hard to spot a giant rock in space?

She wills herself to move further up for a better vantage point, and as if fueled simply by her will, she glides deeper and faster into space. Soon, she's far above the Earth, the planet looking deceptively like a ball she could hold in her hands if she only reached for it.

Her scanning gaze finds the crescent of the moon on the other side. The asteroid had been heading that way before. It must be somewhere in that general direction.

Suddenly, as if her entire field of vision were nothing but a television screen, a thin red circle with four lines around it like a target appears to the left of the moon. Then words and numbers appear just above the target, reading:

*asteroid

*1244 km

*5.2×10^{20} kg

*18 km/s

"Whoa, this suit really is incredible," she whispers, not quite sure what to make of the information in front of her.

Straightening her body, she angles herself toward the little target and wills herself forward.

Moving in space is so weird. She'd always imagined it would be like floating in water, but it's nothing like that. In water, you can feel the liquid surrounding you, holding you in place. It's comforting, almost like being wrapped in a liquid blanket.

Out here, there's literally nothing. Nothing keeping you floating, nothing stopping you from moving in any direction. Her speed picks up faster than she anticipated, and fear chills her insides at the thought of not being able to stop.

Cassandra shakes the emotion away. There's no time for fear, only action.

As she gets closer, the little target in her vision dissipates and the asteroid grows larger and larger, rolling in nothingness as it spirals toward Earth. All around are fragments of rock and debris from the failed missile. A shard of metal races past her, narrowly missing her head, although she knows the suit would have protected her if it'd hit.

She's close enough to the asteroid now that she's sure she can annihilate it with her best sun blast yet. And she really has no time to waste. The closer it gets to Earth, the more chance of collateral damage from the explosion.

Taking in a deep breath, she raises her arms and aims her sweaty palms at the menacing hunk of rock before her. She summons all her strength, all her will, all her fury, ready to unleash everything she's got.

Smack!

Her vision is suddenly spiraling, the crescent moon spinning in and out of her sight like a maniacal Cheshire Cat. It takes her a dizzying moment to realize she's been hit by something. She splays out her limbs and wills herself to stop.

Slowly, the spinning comes to a halt. Now fully in control of her own movement, she looks all around, trying to see what could have hit her. Could it have been a small rock fragment? No. Whatever it was hit her from the opposite direction of the asteroid and debris field.

She sees nothing, aside from the twinkling glints of debris that catch the sun as they spin off into space.

Smack!

This time, the impact came from right in front of her, slamming into her gut and sending her flying backwards.

What the heck?

She bows her back to stop her momentum, and the realization of what's happening suddenly dawns on her.

Skins. The assassins Tristan has always talked about. He said that they could turn invisible.

"Show yourselves!" she yells brazenly, only realizing afterward that her words are trapped inside her suit, unable to carry through the void of space, and they can't hear her.

"Fine," she grumbles, then raises her open palm like a pistol and shoots out little fireballs in every direction. Many disappear into the distance, but a couple of them make contact with seemingly nothing and smash apart.

"Yes!" She hit them!

The blackness behind the two erupted fireballs fills in, bodies encased in shiny white spacesuits seemingly manifesting from nothing. One of them clutches his helmet, the oxygen spraying out of his suit like a geyser, until his struggling stops and he's left floating in place.

Cassandra's breath catches, and a sick feeling rivaling the triumph in her chest as she realizes she just killed him.

She doesn't have time to process either emotion. The

space around her reveals itself to be vastly more populated, with more and more white bodies shedding their invisibility. Six, ten, thirteen, twenty.

Crap! She's completely outnumbered.

No sooner do they expose themselves then they zoom toward her. Pretending this is yet another training session and the Skins are just dodgeballs, Cassandra shoots fireballs at them. But they're so fast, even in space, easily dodging her volleys with Matrix-like speed.

This game continues, Skins serpentining around her as she fires shot after shot. Her ceaseless triggering keeps them at bay, but her periphery is getting smaller and smaller as they gain on her.

Blast! She hits one square in the chest and he explodes like a trash bag. "Ew," she mutters, fighting the urge to gag.

A few shots later and she hits another one, this time turning away from the explosion. She doesn't want to hurt them, especially not like this, but it's them or her.

And it's *not* going to be her.

One breaks through her onslaught and dives at her before she can aim at him. He tackles her, and together they go tumbling. His limbs smack and punch and kick at her, but thanks to her suit, she feels none of it. She hits back, but he's completely unfazed by all her efforts.

More hands grip her, and she has no idea how many of them are on her now. She has to act fast.

She grabs the head of the one who tackled her, and, squeezing her eyes shut, lets her hands heat up. Unwilling to see it, she feels the once solid helmet give and eventually disappear, until his body goes limp against hers and she's able to shove it away.

She twists and turns desperately to grab another. If she has to do this to every single one of them, so be it.

But the many hands on her lock onto her wrists, pulling

them upward even as she blasts at them, essentially rendering her hands—and her fire power—useless.

They don't stop there. They continue to pull on her arms, and it's starting to hurt.

Oh God! They're going to tear her apart!

No! She can't fail! The entire world is depending on her!

Hissing through her teeth, she sends a whimpered prayer into the Universe.

"Help!"

33

TRISTAN

Tristan wishes there was more time to appreciate what's happening right now.

He's flying into space at speeds he never imagined were possible. And what's more, he's doing it with Brielle and Jareth by his side. The Zodiacs are becoming a team.

But there's no time.

One word reached them all simultaneously in HQ, spearing through the speakers. *Help*.

Tristan clenches his jaw, impossibly adding more speed. Cassandra should never have left on her own, no matter how impressive her powers are. What was she thinking? Skins would be surrounding the asteroid. He wouldn't be surprised if they altered the trajectory of the missile so it missed in the first place.

But it was Cassandra's voice that reached them, undeniably desperate and in pain. There's no way she'd be able to fight off a bunch of Skins.

"I see her," says Brielle just as Tristan does.

"Whoa, I can hear you!" Jareth says in wonder.

Holy Pitch, they can all talk to each other? Tristan would

also like to appreciate the technology he just discovered in the suit—the same technology that's now showing him the location of the asteroid and a whole bunch of other cool data —but he can't do that, either.

Not until Cassandra's safe.

The dot that's Cassandra's gold suit steadily grows, becoming a shape that has Brielle gasping. Cassandra's arms are outstretched, her back arched and contorted in pain like she's about to be drawn and quartered.

"Not. Happening," mutters Tristan.

It's time to find out exactly how fast this suit goes.

The stars around him become a blur as he streaks forward, a human missile aimed for Cassandra. A Skin sees him approach and tries to intercept, but Tristan simply uses his momentum to slam the white-suited bastard out of his way. Like a battering ram, he smashes Skin after Skin as if they're little more than bugs.

"There are so many!" calls Jareth, not far behind.

"We can have a party," Tristan calls back.

Cassandra's scream echoes through Tristan's helmet and his muscles tighten. She's almost at snapping point, quite literally.

"We've got you," he says, infusing all the confidence he's not feeling right now into his voice.

Tristan's about to reach Cassandra, but ploughing into either of the Skins holding her arms could result in ending her sooner. If the Skin doesn't let go…they'll take her arm with them.

"Hurry, Tristan!" Cassandra whimpers desperately.

He realizes what he has to do. "You ready to catch me?" he asks her.

"What?"

"Brielle, Jareth. Cover me."

"Always," comes Brielle's immediate response.

The promise injects a burst of much-needed confidence. Bracing himself, Tristan spears straight toward Cassandra.

He crashes into her chest, the impact causing her to collapse in on herself. The Skins holding onto her arms are pulled together like a giant clap, smashing into Tristan and each other. They release their hold, bouncing off and propelling in opposite directions.

Tristan powers away. "Now, Cassandra!"

The blast of light is almost instantaneous, and the Skins disintegrate.

"Never touch me again," Cassandra says fiercely, even though the dudes are dead.

Tristan flies back to her, coming to float in front of her. The Skins have seen what just happened, and they're not happy about it. They flock in, creating a tidal wave of evil.

The next thing Tristan knows, Brielle's beside him, Jareth on the other side. Cassandra shoots forward, coming to hover beside Jareth.

Creating a wall of Zodiac awesomeness.

Except behind the Skins, still miles away but hurtling with impressive speed, is the asteroid. In a few minutes it'll bowl the Zodiacs and Skins out of the way like they're weightless pins.

Tristan braces his legs and clenches his fists. "Time to neutralize the threat."

"I prefer to call it kick some ass," mutters Cassandra.

Tristan shoots forward. "That's what I said."

A second before he hits the Skin coming at him, he twists, extending his leg and ploughing it into the Skin's chest. The chest plate on the man's suit crumples, but Tristan turns away before he can see what the damage will mean. Whether the death will be a quick or a slow one.

More Skins are coming. And each one of them is going to have to die, too.

Brielle appears by his side, executing one hell of an uppercut. When the Skin tries to land his own punch, Brielle executes a smooth backflip, moving out of reach. Impressed, even though there's no time to be, Tristan can't help but admire her style. Despite being encased in a sleek and sexy suit, Brielle knows she's not a strong offensive fighter, so she's staying defensive.

Smart.

"Tristan!"

He spins around, seeing why she just called out his name. Two Skins are coming at him. Fast.

Brielle does another graceful flip, landing behind him. She spins, her back to his, ready to fight.

The Skins attack, two more joining their friends. Tristan kicks and punches, the movements swift and sharp. The suit, with the added protection of Brielle at his back, fuels Tristan's strength. Dealing strike after strike, he absorbs each blow that gets past his defenses, determined that none of them will reach Brielle. And none do. Each time Tristan moves or ducks or spins, Brielle's there with him, as if they're moving as one.

Like they're connected somehow.

To his left, Jareth has created a double of himself. The two forms in their metallic black suits hit and parry so fast, the Skins can't keep up with which one is the real Jareth. The strategy is giving him more time as he formulates his attack.

"Genius!" Tristan calls out to him, not taking his eyes off his foes and the blows he's dealing.

Ploughing his foot through one Skin's chest, he slams the heels of both hands into another's, sending him reeling. Brielle calls another warning, and a quick pirouette and his elbow smashes the Skin's helmet.

Tristan moves fast, Brielle right there with him, but the Skins keep coming. They take the blows, retreat, then attack again, never giving up. Tristan's pulse feels like a freight train, his breath starting to come in gasps. Bolts of light spear through the inky blackness as Cassandra ducks and shoots. There are now three Jareths and even Tristan isn't sure which is the real one.

But with each Skin neutralized, four more seem to replace him.

"Tristan!"

It's Cassandra, her voice full of panic. Looking over, Tristan sees her struggling, even though there doesn't appear to be anyone around her. Jareth quickly covers the distance between them, only to be hurled backward by an unseen force.

It's then that Tristan realizes some of the Skins are still invisible. No wonder it feels as if there's an endless supply of them. Who knows how many are littered throughout the vacuum around them.

Tristan and Brielle hurtle toward her, Tristan ready to slam into Cassandra again, but the Skin releases her before they get there. Blindly, Cassandra shoots off several bolts, but they don't connect.

The Zodiacs contract together, conscious that an unknown number of enemies are now surrounding them.

"You should never have left on your own, Cassandra," Tristan growls in frustration.

Cassandra holds her hands wide and shoots. The bolts of light do little more than look like shooting stars as they hurtle away. "I realize that now."

"I get that you have something to prove, I've been there, okay?" Tristan scans the endless night around them, wondering how they can fix this. The asteroid is now a moving, rolling boulder that feels far too close. "But you almost got yourself killed."

And there's a possibility she might still yet. Along with

the rest of the Zodiacs.

"I said I know!" Cassandra half-shouts. She lets off another bolt, and this one connects with a body. The Skin explodes into space ash.

Tristan squints, realizing he can just make them out, their bodies like stains blocking the starry landscape.

Cassandra spins around, shooting another bolt behind her, just in case. "Tristan! How do we fix this?"

She said *we*. Such a beautiful word.

Tristan points to the asteroid. "We'll keep them busy. You do your thing."

Cassandra hesitates, and Brielle's voice reaches them both.

"Go, Cassandra. This is what you came here to do."

"You're the only one who can," adds Jareth.

Cassandra nods sharply and Tristan can just imagine the hard look of determination on her face right now.

With a last glance at the three of them, she jets away. Tristan sees a blur of black heading toward her and quickly pounces. He snaps the man's neck, throwing the body at the next blur that's coming at him.

"We need to keep their focus on us," Tristan tells the others.

Jareth multiplies once more, this time becoming ten, twenty, fifty. A new wall of Zodiac, but even bigger. Brielle takes her place at Tristan's back again.

By silent agreement, they become a blur of movement. Lashing out at any movement, striking out, over and over.

And over.

Tristan wants to shout at Cassandra to hurry, heck, to please not miss, but he contains himself.

He has no doubt Cassandra knows what's at stake.

That it's only a matter of time before the three remaining Zodiacs are overcome by swarming Skins.

34

CASSANDRA

E verything is riding on this moment.

A horde of invisible jerks are attacking her friends, and no doubt chasing her, as she speeds like a rocket toward the massive asteroid. The asteroid that will destroy everything and everyone if she fails.

Time ticks by at a snail's pace the closer she gets, making her feel like she's moving through cold molasses. Every cruel, judgmental thing her dad has ever said to her replays in her head, every moment she spent curled into a tight protective ball as he whipped her into the shape he wanted, though it was never enough for him.

"You need to be better."

Her pulse kicks into overdrive, and she welcomes the familiar heat in her palms.

"Try harder."

Her hands don't just glow, they spontaneously combust, blazing like miniature suns in the blackness.

"Winners never lose, and you lose all the time."

Anger boils through her veins, forcing her to squeeze her burning eyes shut and clench her jaw so tight that her teeth grind.

"You're such an utter disappointment."

"No, I'm not," she snarls to the voice in her head. She opens her eyes and stops herself in front of the rock that now takes up every bit of her field of vision, straightening her body and puffing out her chest in a position that says, "If you want Earth, you'll have to go through me."

"How was I so unlucky as to adopt the reject of the orphanage?"

Suddenly, all the rage, injured pride, envy of the families of her friends, the hatred warring with the love for her father, and her newfound confidence—all of it—coalesces in her chest and becomes too much to contain.

Thrusting her hands out in front of her, Cassandra unleashes, and a blast of energy greater than anything she's ever experienced erupts, seemingly from her very pores, using her body as a conduit to enter existence.

Lights engulfs her vision, blinding her.

A high-pitched and painfully loud noise pierces her ears, but she's powerless not to hear it.

And the heat is so intense, she fears that her very flesh might burn away.

The explosion rushing out of her threatens to tear her apart, and all she can do is continue to push it out until it's run its course.

Although, there may be nothing left of her by then.

And what if it's not enough, just as her father always said?

Just as abruptly and powerfully as it began, the flood of light, heat and energy stops, like a hose whose faucet has just been shut off.

Cassandra's body goes completely limp, floating in a strange wasteful serenity. Everything is silent, and she realizes now that the shrill noise that had deafened her ears had been her own screaming. For a moment, all she can do is drift in the peace and silence and darkness, unable to even open her eyes. Her mind is fog—no, a void, just like that in which she hovers. And the temptation to stay here, in this internal nothingness, is overwhelming.

Distant voices waft into her silence, irritating her as if she's been woken from a sleep.

But the haste of those voices shocks her into awareness, forcing her eyelids to spring open.

There is nothing in front of her but a thick cloud of dust. Is she still in her mental fog? Are her eyes even open? Or is she dead and lost in some spiritual in-between?

The voices become clearer. Brielle. Tristan. Jareth. What are they saying?

Cassandra struggles to focus on the words.

"…did it! She did it!" one of them is shouting.

"Huh?" she breathes. She blinks, consciousness snapping to full force like an avalanche.

She spins around, taking in all of her surroundings.

The asteroid is gone, a cloud of dust in its place. The Earth is behind her, a magnificent blue orb wafting peacefully in its lazy orbit, ignorant of the epic battle that just saved it and its inhabitants.

And somewhere off to the right, her friends and fellow Zodiac Guardians are still fending off powerful, and now very vengeful, Skins.

The asteroid threat may have been nullified, but the battle isn't over yet. They need her. And she's not playing nice anymore.

"Tristan, Brielle, get close to Jareth quickly," she instructs as she zooms toward them. "Jareth, form a forcefield around the three of you. Oh, and close your eyes."

Their glinting metallic figures gather and join hands, and a strange iridescent bubble materializes around them. White suited assailants intermixed with black smudges against the backdrop of stars swarm in around them.

Cassandra smirks wickedly as she powers forward. They're not going to know what hit them.

Using only a fraction of the power from her blast of moments ago, she detonates another, a wave of light radiating out in all directions from her center. Before her eyes, the white suited bodies and black smudges disintegrate into ashes as the wave pushes through them.

When the light dissipates into the distance, the Zodiacs are finally alone, their only company in the cosmos the Earth, the Moon and the endless stars.

As Cassandra takes in the beauty and peace of this moment, she's sure of one thing.

She will never be afraid of anyone ever again.

35

BRIELLE

They did it! They really did it!

Ok, well, Cassandra was the one who actually destroyed the asteroid, but they stopped Chardis's scheme as a team!

Brielle's heart is fluttering like a freshly caged humming-bird, and it's not just because they're descending back to Earth so quickly that their suits are blazing against the friction of the atmosphere. Heck, she doesn't even care that she has no idea where home is from up here. They could land in the middle of the Atlantic Ocean for all she cares! She's just high on the fact that they succeeded, that the world is safe, and that Tristan is holding her hand just as tightly as she's holding his.

Somehow, Tristan guides them right back to the roof of Alden's mansion where they left from. Thankfully, night has fallen in the time they've been gone, so their descent is masked by darkness.

They land and immediately retract their suits, and as if they collectively couldn't hold back anymore, the four of them hug. Tristan and Jareth share a dude hug as Brielle and Cassandra squeeze each other tightly.

"You were *incredible* up there!" Brielle gushes.

"I know, and it felt unbelievably good!" Cassandra squeals with glee. "I'm so lucky you guys came to rescue my rebel butt." She snickers.

"Luckily, Tristan had a vision as soon as you left." Brielle thanks pitch that the bad vision didn't come true, squeezing Cassandra harder.

They withdraw, and Cassandra goes to hug Jareth as Brielle and Tristan simultaneously turn to each other. Without hesitating, they close the distance between them like two magnets pulled together and wrap their arms around one another.

Like two puzzle pieces, they fit perfectly into each other. The next movement is so natural, instinctive. Almost primal. Before Brielle can stop herself, her lips find Tristan's.

Or do his find hers? Or does the Universe finally correct some grievous imbalance and suddenly everything feels good and right?

His lips part at the same moment she opens hers to take a breath, and the sweet smell of him beckons her tongue forward to sample his taste. His own hungrily meets hers, caressing, tangling, wrestling into euphoric submission.

Every pent up emotion, every repressed urge she's denied herself since they met breaks free of its restraints and revels in the feel of him, gets lost in the feel of him, until she can't tell where she ends and he begins.

Maybe this isn't real. Maybe they really did die at the hands of the Skins and the asteroid, because this is Heaven. It's utter bliss!

They part for a moment, each in desperate need of catching their breath. Their eyes meet, and for a beautiful, glorious instant, Tristan's gaze is filled with the same unbridled joy and desire as her own.

But as she watches, the light dwindles, his brow slowly hitches upward, and suddenly, he wrenches himself away from her.

Confused and wounded, her body stinging from the sudden removal of his as if she's been horribly sliced open, Brielle stands there, shocked into paralysis.

Her brows pucker in question, and in response Tristan shakes his head and sprints to the roof access door, leaving the three of them in dead silence.

Brielle suddenly realizes that Jareth and Cassandra are there, and that they saw the whole thing. A shamed blush conquers every inch of her skin, but she still can't move. Her eyes sheepishly wander to Cassandra, afraid of the judgment she might find there.

But the golden-maned barbie face only looks both outraged and encouraging. "What are you still standing here for? Go after him!"

Spurred into action like a racehorse by a gunshot, Brielle sprints to the door and leaps down the stairs after him. He's leaning against the wall at the bottom, broodingly rubbing his chin.

"Tristan?" Her voice is small, pleading. Desperate.

He kicks away from the wall and rubs his hands over his face and through his hair. "I'm so sorry," he groans. "That should never have happened."

His denial is like a slap in the face. No, a punch in the gut.

No. A stab in the heart.

Her head shakes of its own accord, as if her entire body is rebelling against this rejection. "Why not?" she demands, the volume of her voice now echoing in the small space.

He turns to her, his eyes begging for her to understand. But she can't.

"Because we can't be together," he all but shouts, throwing his hands up.

She flinches, hot tears threatening to break over the dam of her eyelids. Her natural inclination is to bow out of this argument and accept defeat. But she refuses to let this go. Not this time.

"Why do you keep running from this?" she asks, an edge to her voice. "I know you feel the same way I do. I felt it in that kiss, if not the countless times we've been alone together. You kissed me, too, Tristan. Tell me I'm wrong."

Letting out a shaky, defeated groan, he hangs his head and slumps his shoulders looking like he's ready to fall to the floor. "You're not wrong," he whimpers. "I... I do feel for you, but we can't." He looks up at her with desperation. "I have a soulmate out there waiting—"

"So what?" she asks with a shrug.

"So what?" he repeats with insult.

"What if you never find her?" Brielle continues. "What if her pod crashed upon landing and she just isn't out there? Are you going to hold me at arm's length your entire life waiting for someone who might never come, who might not even exist? I could make you so happy..." Her voice hitches, and she can't continue in case she breaks down in a sobbing fit from which she'll never recover.

He stares at her for a long, quiet moment, his jaw clenching and unclenching. "It's not about how happy you could make me," he says solemnly, then looks away. "It's about how miserable I could make you."

Reflexively, she rushes to his side. "Tristan, you could never make me miserable," she reassures, pouring her heart into her words, her soft touches on his shoulders.

"Yes, I could. If we start this, and then we find her."

Oh. Her eyes widen, and her arms fall away from him.

"I refuse to break your heart like that."

"So you'd rather break it now," she states flatly.

"It's the only thing I can do," he says. "It's what's best for the Zodiacs, and believe it or not, it's what's best for you."

She shakes her head in defiance. "Fine, if that's what you want." Then she turns on her heel and storms out before he can see her tears fall.

How did this evening go so quickly from victorious bliss to complete and utter tragedy?

JACK

21:22

Jack watches the replay of the asteroid's destruction from Nebula's office.

Three people were there. All in suits that have never been seen before.

With no way to recognize the people wearing them.

And yet, he knows without a doubt who at least one of them was. Probably two.

Tristan. And Brielle.

They're Zodiac Heirs, whatever the hell that means. And although they saved the Earth this time, their very existence is a threat. Because they're not human.

They're aliens.

Jack presses a button on the console in front of him.

"Yes, Director?" asks a cool, female voice.

"I'll be sending out a message to all Nebula operatives." Discovering they're stationed all over the world had been a pleasant surprise. "It needs to go out with the highest importance."

"It will be encrypted accordingly."

Jack lifts his finger off the button, terminating the call.

Once that email is read by every Nebula member, all eyes are going to be on Tristan and his friends.

The truce is null and void.

36

CASSANDRA

Riding on a wave of electrifying adrenaline, Cassandra drives home. She's never felt this good in her entire life! And she won't let anything bring her down.

"Where on Earth have you been?" her father barks as soon as she enters the front door. His arms are crossed, and the little vein on his left temple is engorged and throbbing. He looks positively terrifying.

But Cassandra's not afraid anymore.

"I was with Brielle," she responds, casually hanging her purse on the coat rack. And technically, she wasn't on Earth. She indulges in a private smirk before she turns back to him.

His face turns a darker shade of red. Apparently, her answer was not good enough for him. "I called you several dozen times! Why didn't you answer? I was getting ready to call the police."

"I was a little...preoccupied," she says, remembering the awesome showdown in space from earlier tonight, and a spike of thrill shoots through her. "Besides, I'm surprised you care, seeing as I'm such a disappointment." She bravely meets his steely gaze, even though that little girl inside her wants to curl into a ball.

No more.

His mouth falls open, and for a moment, he looks utterly shocked.

The surprise quickly turns into rage, and he points a dagger-like finger in her face. "How dare you speak to me like that! Just because the world is ending doesn't mean you can disrespect me!"

She swallows, refusing to flinch every time the volume of his voice spikes. "The world isn't ending. Haven't you heard? The asteroid has been destroyed."

Disbelief blankets his face.

He really didn't know. He really thought the asteroid was still heading for Earth. Has the news not gotten out yet?

"No, it wasn't," he says, the register of voice coming back down. "The missile hit it wrong. The asteroid is now hurtling towards Earth. And since the news broke, I've had no idea where you were or how to find you!"

Now it's her turn to be shocked. He was actually worried about her?

Her bravado wanes, her shoulders relaxing a bit. "I'm sorry, Dad. I was watching the news with my friends—"

"Sorry isn't good enough!" he snaps, returning to his usual sternness. "Now we may not have enough time to get to the ship! We had to wait for you, and now we may all die!" He rakes his fingers through his usually well-kept hair, which looks as though he's been doing this all afternoon.

She stiffens once more, feeling foolish for letting herself think he actually cared about her. He just wanted to save himself. Although, props for him for not just completely leaving her behind.

She rolls her eyes. "No one is going to die. Like I said, the asteroid has been destroyed. The first missile missed, but sounds like someone else launched another missile. No more asteroid."

He narrows his eyes at her, as if he thinks she's lying.

"Check your phone." She juts her chin to the rectangular lump in his slacks pocket.

After another moment of staring, he slowly pulls out his phone and flips through it. His eyes gradually grow wider and wider, until he sharply inhales. "Oh my god, you're right!" His fingers comb through his hair again, this time in relief.

"See. All good." She tries to slip past him, but he cuts her off by side-stepping in front of her.

"Oh, no, no, no." His familiar shadow looms over her, and she knows what's coming. "Asteroid or no asteroid, your flagrant disrespect for your parents and reckless negligence of this family's well-being will not be tolerated." His fingers fumble with his belt buckle.

Her pulse races in remembered fear, but she pushes through it.

"No."

"What?" he hisses, pulling the leather out of the buckle.

"You will not touch me ever again," she declares clearly and slowly.

He grabs her wrist and holds it up in exhibition. "The hell I won't! You are my daughter, and you need discipline!"

"No!" She yanks her arm out of his grip. "If you ever raise a finger to me in anger again, I will go to every news station in the state with my justified claims of child abuse."

His eyes widen as if she just slapped him. "No one would believe you. You have no proof."

"As if the scars, welts and bruises aren't enough proof, it won't matter if they believe me or not." She flares a daring brow. "The story itself will be a scandal. You would be ruined."

The first spark of fear she's ever seen from her father flashes in his gray eyes, and his complexion pales slightly.

He swallows and takes a step backward, giving her space to move freely. She takes it and walks past him without looking back.

Elation bubbles through Cassandra's chest. She actually stood up to her father! Somehow, this feels like an even bigger victory than saving the planet from a deadly asteroid.

That's two epics wins for the day.

Now time for a well-deserved hot shower to celebrate!

Cassandra walks into the diner, the bright sunlight flooding in behind her.

It's a beautiful day! The sun is shining, the streets are quiet and clear—if a little scattered with trash and broken glass here and there. For the most part, the day feels… normal. Like the world didn't almost end yesterday.

"There she is!" Jareth calls from a booth.

Veronica hops to her feet, looking at Cassandra with school girl crush eyes. Cassandra raises a curious brow as she joins them.

"Omigod!" Veronica squeals, throwing her arms exuberantly around Cassandra. "Did you really blow it up?" she asks in a strained whisper.

Cassandra looks around before answering, then says with a proud nod, "You bet I did."

There's another squeal as they sit down. Veronica hunches over the table and continues to whisper. "Oh man, I wish I could have seen you in action! Jareth says you were amazing! Like Wonder Woman."

"If Wonder Woman were a walking flamethrower," Jareth adds with a wink.

"Wonder Woman wishes she was as awesome as me." Cassandra intentionally flips her hair back.

They share a laugh.

Cassandra is loving the accolades. She's never felt better. Jareth and Veronica seem lighter, too. In fact, even the staff behind the counter are dancing to the crackly music of a small old radio. It's the buoyancy of knowing you've just been given another chance at life after coming so close to death.

"Good morning, guys." Cassandra turns in time to see Brielle lowering into the booth next to her.

The three of them return her greeting. Brielle is wearing a smile, but Cassandra can tell it's only skin deep. It's almost like there's a cloud over her head, shading her from the beauty of this bright new day that's affecting everyone else.

"Is everything okay?" Cassandra asks, hushing her voice slightly.

Brielle shrugs. "It will be." Then she picks up a menu and holds it in front of her face. Before the laminated paper covers her, Cassandra catches the glint of a hovering tear.

Cassandra has no idea what happened between Brielle and Tristan after they left the room. When she and Jareth had come down from the roof, neither love bird was in sight. And Cassandra didn't want to pry with invasive text messages, no matter how much she wanted to know if the two made amends. Judging by Brielle's somber semblance, probably not.

Stupid Tristan.

Where is he, by the way? Cassandra looks around. He should have come with Jareth.

"When's Tristan gonna get here?" she asks Jareth.

Jareth eyes flick to Brielle's menu and back to Cassandra. "He's…tied up with something this morning, so he's not coming."

Cassandra sighs and shakes her head slightly. *Yep. Stupid Tristan.*

"Not coming to our victory meal?" Veronica scoffs. "What's more important than this right now?"

Jareth just shrugs dismissively, and Cassandra wonders if Veronica will see through his façade.

"Oh, look, look! It's on the news!" squeals one of the girls behind the counter.

"I told you it wasn't fake!" says the Hispanic male server to the others.

Their commotion has the four of them looking at the TV in the corner. Even Brielle looks over her menu.

Then drops it.

As if in a chorus, the four of them gasp.

"Oh. My. God!" Veronica breathes.

"This can't be happening," Jareth says with his hand over his mouth.

On the screen is shaking footage of three figures shooting up through the clouds.

One pink. One black. One purple.

"This video was taken by an airline passenger yesterday only moments before the unexplained explosion of the asteroid," reports the voice of Sofia of Channel 2 News as the video shrinks to box in the upper right corner next to her face. "No government agency has yet come forward with an explanation, but social media is flooding with talk of…superheroes."

"Oh no." Brielle drops her face into her hands.

They were seen.

No, worse. They were filmed.

Cassandra curses under breath, mostly at herself. If she had only waited for them all to go together, the three of them might not have passed that plane.

The Zodiacs aren't a secret anymore.

TRISTAN

"Here you go, love. It's on the house," Madge purrs as she holds out a fro-yo with all his favorite toppings, even Gummy Bears.

Tristan looks up from where he was nursing his head like he has a hangover.

It sure as pitch feels like one. There's the heavy regret somersaulting in his gut. The pounding head.

The knowledge that he wants to do it all over again.

Except he can't. He never should've kissed Brielle.

And he never will again.

No matter how mind-blowing it was.

He takes the fro-yo, even though he's not hungry. "No Oreos?" he jokes half-heartedly.

Madge winks. "I've stashed them for the next global disaster."

Tristan tries to laugh, even summons up a chuckle, but all he does is choke. His body's even rebelling against fake happiness.

Madge thumps him on the back. "No need to worry, love," she soothes. "We're all going to be fine."

"There's no way you can say that."

Chardis's asteroid may have been destroyed, but the Zodiacs are no longer a secret.

And there are still nine more Guardians to find.

And Tristan kissed Brielle.

It was the worst thing he could've done. By giving in to the undeniable attraction he feels for her, he's undermined the fragile foundation the Zodiacs have established. He betrayed the very people he's trying to unite.

And the worst part is, he now knows what he's missing out on. Sweet joy. Sizzling desire. A sense of being…whole.

How the hell does he stay away from her now?

Madge crosses her arms. "Yeah, I do know, actually. Everything's gonna be okay."

Tristan shakes his head. "I have a feeling there's more to come."

"Of course there is, honey!" Madge waves a hand, obviously unaware she's dismissing the threat of Earth's destruction. "But we've got people like you looking out for us."

Tristan stills even though he doesn't mean to. Madge would've seen the footage of the Zodiacs. Surely, she hasn't connected the smattering of evidence she's been privy to—a boy dropping off a thumbdrive, Tristan saving her from the dude with the bat…the footage of the Zodiacs. Still, it would mean she's connected dots that hail from different zipcodes.

She leans forward, the wrinkles around her eyes deepening as she narrows them. "Your secret's safe with me," she promises solemnly.

And yet, she seems to have reached a conclusion that Tristan is more than he seems…

"Madge—"

She presses a finger to his lips and Tristan's so surprised, he merely sits there.

"I wanted you to know…"

Instantly, Tristan wishes he'd pulled away. As much as he doesn't want to offend Madge, he also doesn't want her to get the wrong idea.

She smiles as she removes her finger and withdraws. "You got yourself a lifetime of frozen desserts. On the house."

Tristan smiles gratefully. Madge is practically mothering him, and that feels kind of good right now.

She leans forward, shimmying a shoulder in front of his face as her eyebrows dance in time to the movement. "Or if you even need a shoulder to lean on, Hero Boy…"

This time, Tristan grins. There's the Madge he knows and loves. "I'll keep that in mind."

He jams his spoon in his fro-yo, hoping a sugar hit might lift his mood. "And I don't know what ideas you've got in that pretty head of yours, but you're wrong. My dad taught me Jiu-Jitsu from a young age."

Which is true. It's just that Zarius taught him that along with several other martial arts. So he could defend the world from evil.

Madge frowns as she processes the explanation for Tristan's fighting skills. Maybe it will be enough to undermine her not-so-crazy theory.

"Tristan?"

Tristan turns around at the sound of his name. The voice is familiar, but not one he can place.

A boy is standing just inside the door. Tristan's eyes widen as he shoots to his feet. It's the kid who gave him the thumb drive! The one who warned of the black hole!

He deliberately unwinds his muscles, trying to look relaxed. He can't afford for the boy to get away from him this time. "Hey kid, great to see you again. What's your name?"

The boy grins. "Wouldn't you like to know."

Before Tristan can say anything else, the boy lifts his hand.

"I was told to give you this."

Knowing the moment he takes the thumb drive, the kid will disappear, Tristan leaps forward. He needs to know who he's working for.

But the boy must be expecting it, because he winds his arm back and sends the thumb drive flying through the air. Instinctively, Tristan changes trajectory so he can catch it. There's no doubt in his mind that it contains valuable information.

Except by the time the thumb drive has landed in Tristan's palm, the boy is gone.

"Dammit," Tristan mutters, shooting after him.

He crashes through the door, and a teen on a skateboard leaps backward as Tristan almost bowls him over.

"Hey, watch it, dude!

"Sorry," Tristan mumbles, eyes already scanning to see which direction the kid has run.

Except the boy's nowhere to be seen, which is impossible. Tristan frowns. Unless he's a Skin.

It's then that he sees a black, unmarked car zooming away. A small hand is visible waving through the back window.

"Double dammit," Tristan mutters.

He's half considering running after it when Madge's voice comes from behind him. "Like I said," she whispers loudly. "Your secret's safe with me."

With a knowing look followed by another little shoulder shimmy, Madge disappears back inside.

"Triple dammit."

Frowning hard, Tristan looks down at the small, silver rectangle in his hand. Another thumb drive, no doubt meant for Zarius.

A second later, he's jogging. His heart thuds the whole

way home, but not with exertion. A part of him doesn't want to know what's on it.

The house is quiet when he enters, but Tristan expected it to be. Jareth has been spending even more time with Veronica after everything they've been through, and Tristan can't blame him. Brielle's been avoiding him since their... kiss, and Tristan can't blame her for that, either.

He couldn't give her any more mixed messages if he tried.

Down in HQ, Tristan walks to the nearest computer. He hesitates as he's about to slip the thumb drive into the computer port, but not for the reasons he did last time he was given one.

This time he knows it's not a virus or a bomb. But he's just as nervous.

If this is anything like the last message, it's about to change everything.

Clenching his jaw, he slots it in. Just like the first time, the screen flickers then turns blue. Then white. Alden's technology gives it the all-clear.

And then the words appear.

The wormhole is complete.

Tristan lets out his breath. That's nothing he doesn't know. The wormhole would've needed to be complete for the asteroid to come through.

Freezing, Tristan watches the words disappear, realizing there will be more. If the wormhole is complete, then—

A single asteroid was only the beginning.

Ready for the next installment in the Zodiac Guardians series?
Check out TAURUS DIVIDED!

http://mybook.to/TaurusDivided

TAURUS DIVIDED

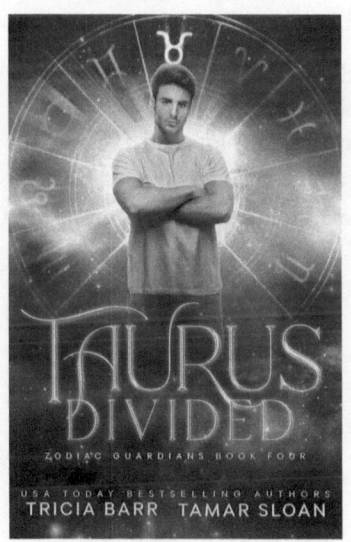

Twelve teens. One task.
Save the Universe.

Logan owes everything to the man who adopted him. Jack
Cadbury loved and raised him as his own and Logan's deter-

mined to follow in his footsteps—become an FBI agent and prove his father's theories are true.

Dating Cassandra is his in. The beautiful blonde is obviously connected to Tristan and Brielle. As Logan gets closer to the Zodiacs than Jack ever hoped, he's recruited into the FBI's secret organization—Nebula.

But deep in Nebula's bowels, Logan finds a pod. The pod he arrived in when he crashed to Earth. And the pod has a message for him…

As Logan learns he's everything his father wants to destroy, the Zodiacs discover Chardis has spies and traitors everywhere. Evil is resurfacing, determined to divide and destroy the fragile team.

Will Logan choose the father who loves him, or his new family who are desperately trying to save the Universe? What's more, will he betray Cassandra, the girl he wasn't supposed to fall in love with?

Fans of paranormal and sci-fi romance will love this Sailor Moon meets Avengers series from USA Today Best-Selling authors Tricia Barr and Tamar Sloan!

Grab your copy HERE!

mybook.to/TaurusDivided

MORE EPIC ROMANCE TO FALL IN LOVE WITH!

ALSO BY TAMAR SLOAN

PRIME PROPHECY SERIES

KEEPERS OF THE GRAIL

KEEPERS OF THE CHALICE

KEEPERS OF THE LIGHT

KEEPERS OF EXCALIBUR

DESTINED DEMIGODS

ELEMENTAL GAMES

THE SOVEREIGN CODE

THE THAW CHRONICLES

ALSO BY TRICIA BARR

THE MATING GAMES

THE BOUND ONE SERIES

THE AMARANT SERIES

SHIFTER ACADEMY

HEAVENLY SINNERS

ABOUT THE AUTHORS

By day, Tricia is a full time mom to two beautiful girls and a wife/business partner to a handsome hard-working husband. By night—and nap times—she's a USA Today Bestselling Author of unique and thrilling teen and adult fantasies inspired by her vivid, somewhat creepy dreams and her own adventures around the world.

Tamar hasn't decided whether she's a psychologist who loves writing, or a writer with a lifelong fascination with psychology. She must've been someone pretty awesome in a previous life (past life regression indicates a Care Bear), because she gets to do both. When not reading, writing, or working with teens, Tamar can be found with her husband and two sons enjoying country life in their small slice of the Australian bush.